THE Kissing GAME

LOVE ALIVE 1

ANITA DAVIS

ISBN-10: 1-946721-12-3
ISBN-13: 978-1-946721-12-9

Books may be purchased in quantity by contacting the author Anita Davis:
Set Apart Publishing
PO Box 39229
Chicago, IL 60639
or by email at authoranitadavis@gmail.com

ACKNOWLEDGMENTS

Thanks to my great friends, authors, Sherelle Green (your continued encouragement for this book's release has been appreciated and needed) and Angela Seals, I wrote this book back in 2017 with one goal in mind but plans change. ☺

Thank you to my author-sister, Suzette Harrison and my betas, Latrease, Arnesia, and Midnight. You all are great.

I hope you all enjoy Miriam and Shawn's story.

A kiss is a secret told to the mouth instead of the ear; kisses are the messages of love and tenderness.

~Ingrid Bergman

1

"Pass me the container." Miriam motioned to her best friend, Dana.

"Hunh?" Dana's smooth, chocolate face scrunched up as she tapped her ear.

"You have your hearing aids in. You can hear me. I said, give me that." Miriam pointed to what Dana was holding.

"Oh." Dana giggled. "Wait your turn." She pulled the gallon of cookie dough ice cream further out of Miriam's reach as they both sat on the plush, floor rug. She scooped a heap of the hard, yet decadent substance from the tub before hesitantly handing it to Miriam.

Miriam's head dropped further and further into the tub.

Dana laughed.

Miriam's head popped up. "Really? You couldn't

even save me some?" She placed the container back on the floor between her and Dana only to have Dana pick it up and scrape it for the last liquefied spoonful.

Miriam got up from the floor and flopped down on the couch behind her and propped her head on a pile of plush throw pillows.

She was in the middle of watching an architecture documentary, and although it bored Dana, it was time they spent together. Dana sat through it, intermittently trying to change the channel only to have Miriam fuss until she changed it back.

"It's sad that on yet another Friday night we're gorging on ice cream and pizza and watching these dreaded documentaries you enjoy so much instead of out claiming the town as our own or on dates." Dana sighed as she moved to lay on the couch perpendicular to the one Miriam lay on.

"Whatever, you know architecture is my thing, so any show talking about it gets my attention. And I'm perfectly fine enjoying my Friday night on this couch and with this pillow." She smiled and inhaled the fresh linen scent of the pillow she hugged close to her chest. "You know I've been focused at work, trying to put myself in the position to make senior executive architect." She smiled, thinking about her dream position. "Mr. Pierce wants to meet with me soon. With his S.E.A. retiring to Florida, I think the opportunity has come along for me to take his place. Which means there's no time to relax. It's time to turn the dial all the way up."

"Turn your fire up any higher, and you'll incinerate yourself," Dana said as she shook her head and her full, naturally curly hair whipped in the air.

"Whatever. I have so much work to do to secure this promotion, but just for tonight, I'm going to try and enjoy myself."

"And you call this enjoying yourself?" Dana fanned her hand across the open box of pizza and emptied containers of ice cream and cookies sprawled out on the floor.

"Yes." Miriam assured her with a head nod.

"Mimi, I really wish you would learn the definition of fun."

"You don't need me to have fun. You could've gone out tonight and left me here, alone, to enjoy my version of fun," Miriam said as she stared at her big TV screen.

"You're right. I don't need you to go out and have fun, but I do need money to do it."

Miriam laughed. She rolled over on her stomach and braced her chin on the pillow underneath it. "So, that audition you had didn't work out the other day?"

"Audition?" Dana's five foot eight, slim yet muscular frame rolled over until she was face up. Her shoulder-length twist out draped over the pillow, making its taupe hue disappear. She pulled her knees to her chest as she continued talking. "I didn't bother taking off work from the temp agency. I had a feeling it wouldn't pan out." She began stretching out one leg at a time. Being a dancer, she was always doing some type of movement to keep herself agile.

"Dana, you say dance is your passion, but lately, you haven't been acting like it. What's up?"

"I don't want to talk about it." Dana quickly changed the channel until she heard the word "love" and paused her surfing. She sat up and leaned forward as if the motion would drown out Miriam's pleas to return the TV to the documentary. "Shhhh." She hushed Miriam and sat Indian style on the couch as she looked at the screen.

Miriam shook her head at Dana but rested on her side and tuned in to the host.

"...Yes, that's right ladies and gentlemen, the show everyone's talking about, The Kissing Game, is coming to Chicago, and we're looking for you to participate. We're certain you've heard of love at first sight, but what about love at first kiss? Do you think one kiss can determine your compatibility with a person? Tried online dating and it didn't work out? Just haven't met the *one*? So then it won't hurt to give 'The Kissing Game' a try." The commercial continued as Dana's smile powered up to high wattage, and she stared at Miriam.

"We should totally do that show." Dana clapped her

hands in glee.

"Um, no, *we* shouldn't. You can if you want to, but I'm not."

"Why not, Mimi? It's not like you have men lined up at the door."

"And I'm fine with that," Miriam clapped back. "Do you not see how busy I am all of the time with work, especially trying to position myself for the promotion? A man is not on my radar now."

"He should be. Then maybe you'd loosen up." Dana's eyes rested on Miriam, and her head cocked to the side.

Miriam didn't bother to dignify Dana's quip with a response.

"You've proven yourself already Mimi. There's no need to work yourself into the ground anymore as hard as you do."

"That's what you say, but I know otherwise." Miriam's mood had sobered. Dana wasn't right. She had so much more to prove.

She got up from the couch. "I'm gonna go and take a relaxing bubble bath and then turn in for the night." She dropped a throw pillow on Dana's face in jest. "Can you clean up that mess for me?" She laughed as she headed to the master bedroom of the massive condo she owned in the Southside neighborhood of Bronzeville in Chicago.

Dana came from under the pillow to be heard loud

and clear. "Just because you've let me live here with you at an amazingly discounted rate since I left California doesn't mean I'm your slave." Dana chuckled as she began to clean up their mess.

2

Marveling at construction sites had always been Miriam's thing for as long as she could remember. She didn't want to wear a hardhat and hammer away at things, she wanted to be the one to birth the design of the buildings she'd studied as a kid. Like the statuesque museums she visited with her elementary school or the varying houses and commercial properties she rode past on the bus in high school, down to the massive brick building she stared at from her living room window whenever her mother was in one of her drunken states.

Miriam would drown out her mother's rants as she imagined the design of each floor in the three-story nursing home across the street from her apartment building. It didn't matter if it wasn't the most modern building that she had seen in her short years on earth, it had character. Its sliding windows open during the summer months allowed many of the stationary residents the chance to smell the fresh, city air. Its tall, white columns framing the entryway seemed so inviting to the elders she often saw returned to it daily.

Her apartment on the fourth floor gave her an almost aerial vantage point to see that the nursing home was shaped like an "L." It always made her think of the word love. She wanted to design structures that provided a love type feeling to people no matter what the building would be used for.

She wanted people to be in awe of her designs.

That desire lingered with her and ushered her right into Cornell University in Ithaca, New York where she majored in architecture. She was an exceptional student, graduating with honors and was more than happy to interview with the top architecture firm in Chicago. She shared their vision of seeing projects through from the architecture, to the civil engineering, down to the type of tile that would be laid on the floors. The C.E.O. and founder, Mark Pierce, of Pierce Industries, saw her passion for architecture and after interviewing her knew she aligned perfectly with the vision of his company.

She'd been with the firm for the past ten years, gleaning from those she could and making an imprint on the company, which brought her to the meeting with Mr. Pierce.

"Hi. Miriam, right?" his personal assistant said.

"Yes." Miriam smiled.

Valerie, the assistant, picked her phone up to buzz Mr. Pierce. After a quick convo with him, she ended the call and redirected her attention to Miriam. "Mr. Pierce is ready to see you now. You can go in."

Miriam walked up to the door and took a deep breath before twisting the knob. She had a feeling that this was the meeting she had been waiting on. The one that would change her life. Get her the promotion she had been eyeing since she joined the company. The one that would show that she had value, unlike what she'd been told growing up.

Her smile radiated from her heart as she walked through the door, but her heart almost stopped when she saw Shawn Lafayette sitting in a chair in front of Mr. Pierce's desk.

She thought it'd be a one on one meeting with him and what she hoped would be the moment he promoted her, but Shawn's presence altered her dream for the time being.

"So good to see you, Miriam. Come, join us." Mr. Pierce stood but remained behind his desk as his outstretched hand beckoned Miriam to take the empty seat next to Shawn.

All six feet and four inches of Shawn's solid frame stood as well, waiting for Miriam to take her seat before he rejoined his.

"Hello, gentlemen." She gave Shawn an apprehensive

smile before she turned to give Mr. Pierce a gracious one.

Mr. Pierce chuckled as he watched Miriam shift in her seat, somewhat angling her body away from Shawn. "I imagine you're shocked to see Shawn here as well, aren't you?"

She paused to choose her words carefully. "I admit, sir, I am."

"I'm sorry, have you two officially met? To my knowledge, you all haven't worked on any projects or accounts together, right?"

Neither Miriam nor Shawn could get a word in edgewise before Mr. Pierce continued, "I mean, I don't think I'd have two of my best work on the same project at the same time. I'd make sure you each were head of different projects to ensure the success of both. Oh, listen to me going on and on. Have you two met?"

"Not officially. As you've said, we've been busy over the years with our own projects, and we haven't had the opportunity to get acquainted with one another." Shawn's rugged, deep voice answered as he looked over at Miriam with a hint of admiration.

Miriam hid her annoyance for him responding before she did. It was supposed to be her chance to shine with Mr. Pierce, and yet Shawn was equally consuming, if not, overtaking her time with her boss with just his presence.

"You're two of my best. It's a pity you all aren't more acquainted with one another. Well, Shawn

Lafayette, meet Miriam Caldwell. Miriam, meet Shawn."

Shawn stretched his arm out, and his massive and strong hand engulfed her soft one as he firmly but gently gripped it into a handshake.

He genuinely smiled at her, but she ended the for-show pleasantry abruptly when her hazel eyes noticed the way his almond-shaped eyes highlighted the chestnut hue of his irises. They intrigued her in a way she didn't have time to dwell on. She'd never even been that close to him before to notice the peculiarity about him.

"Okay, now that we have the introductions out of the way, I'll get straight to the point. As you all may have heard, Peter Garrison is leaving us and retiring to Florida. With that being the case, we need a new senior executive architect. And as you all know, that's as close to partner as anyone would ever make in this firm." He chuckled. "Really, you two are my top choices."

Shawn smiled heartily.

Miriam smiled, but her happiness was overshadowed by the knowledge that she wouldn't so easily be given the position. She was clearly in competition with Shawn for the promotion. Hadn't she already done enough for the company to prove that she was indeed the best candidate for the job?

"You both are incredibly great at what you do. If I could, I would promote both of you, but since I can't, the one who wins over Barry Schaeffer, a billionaire from Manhattan, with their design proposal for the overhaul of his properties will be promoted to senior executive architect. He just bought a chain of hotels and wants to completely revamp them and make his mark in the hotel industry.

Miriam was lost in glee at the news of what the project would offer her—yet another chance to show her prowess seeing a building through from its foundation being laid to the choice of pillows that would lay on the bed of each of the suites. The clearing of a throat to the left of her squashed her merriment and brought her back to the gnawing reality that the promotion and the project wasn't hers just yet. She dared to look over at Shawn as Mr. Pierce relayed more details to them.

As she eyed Shawn, she admitted that she didn't know much about him. Up until that point, she refused to succumb to the reality that he was fine, had a great sense of style, and given the way his tailored suit hugged his frame, was muscular in all the right places.

But all of that was beside the point.

She was social with her coworkers on an as-needed basis. During times she interacted with others outside of her immediate team, she learned of a few female coworkers that doted on him. They all seemed mesmerized by his deep brown skin and his perfect smile, but none of that mattered to her since she'd spent the past ten years of her days and nights focused on providing beyond stellar results for the clients afforded to her with any project she worked on.

Mr. Pierce's chipper voice interrupted her invasive perusal of Shawn.

He pushed a file folder towards each of them. "My assistant emailed you what's in the files I just handed you, but I had her printout just a few specs on Mr. Schaeffer and the properties he's acquired to brand as his own. As with any other projects you all undertake, it's now your turns to do your research and start collecting data and specs to build your proposals around. "He stood, which prompted both Miriam and Shawn to stand also. "I'm certain with what you each have done in the past, you'll make my decision tough for me." He chuckled. "But good luck to the both of you, nonetheless. Enjoy the rest of your day."

"You too. And thank you for this opportunity." Miriam gave him an earnest smile and shook his hand. His pasty complexion was only a shade lighter than hers.

Shawn quickly said his farewell to Mr. Pierce and rushed ahead of Miriam to open the door for her. He pulled the door in towards him and smiled as he stretched his hand forward to her. "Here, you go first." He stared down at her. He had no choice, his stature towered her five feet and eight inches.

"Thanks," she said without looking at him as she walked out the door.

Honestly, she was a nice person but couldn't bring herself to be more cordial, say anything more than what she had to Shawn. Although she never judged a book by its cover, the fact that she was in competition with Shawn made him her enemy for the time being.

3

She had no idea why her car was parked outside of the apartment building she grew up in. Maybe her optimism led her there. Maybe this time when she tried to build the bridge with her mother, Maxine Caldwell wouldn't burn it the minute she opened the door and her mouth. Or maybe Miriam was a glutton for punishment.

Whatever brought her there made her pass through the wrought iron gate and take the memorized seventy-five paces to her mother's entrance in the co-way building and push the button.

A three-minute wait, with her hands clutching her purse and no response made her pivot on her heels to head back to her car, but a slurred voice came across the intercom.

"Who is it?"

Miriam glanced at her watch and mumbled, "6 p.m. Of course, she wouldn't be sober this time of day." She turned back towards the door, cleared her throat and said, "It's me, ma."

"Dammit."

The door buzzed, signaling Miriam to enter. She took the carpeted stairs one at a time until she made it to the fourth floor.

She lifted her hand to knock on the heavy, dark wooden door, but it pulled open, and the strong scent of gin hit her nose.

Maxine didn't even bother to speak before she turned and walked back to her favorite spot on the right end of the couch.

Miriam walked through the door and closed it. From a quick scan of the place, nothing had changed. Including her mother.

Maxine sat there, gripping her cup and staring at the TV. Miriam realized that her mother never really watched the TV because she never laughed, cried, smiled or reacted to anything on the screen. She just stared at it.

Glancing at the picture of Chicago's only black mayor, Harold Washington, on the wall, Miriam thought back to how her mother never purchased any of her school pictures, let alone put any pictures of her up around the house.

The place was kempt, with nothing too out of place.

No dirty dishes stacked high and no clothes strewn all over, but looking at the gloom of the apartment and remembering her sad time spent there, the feel of it all was enough to make her speak up as she sat in one of the armchairs next to the couch. She wanted to get on to what she had gone there for. "How are you, ma?"

Maxine grunted.

"Ma, how are you?"

"Dammit Miriam, don't start that nagging me."

Miriam never understood how her trying to hold a conversation with her mother equated to nagging for Maxine.

But then again, she did get it. Maxine never wanted her, and it showed in every action and inaction she displayed.

Taking a deep breath before she spoke again helped Miriam to keep her tears at bay. "Ma, I'm not trying to nag you, I just stopped by to talk to you, see how you're doing."

Maxine splayed her thin arms out wide. "You see me? You see me? I'm doing just damn fine." She sat back snickering and crossed one bony leg over the other.

Miriam studied her pecan hued mother. The years hadn't been kind to her, and it wasn't solely because of aging. Her mother was only fifty-five years old, not too old to not look stunning and lively. She knew it was because of the fifths of gin her mother downed daily that had dried up her skin, thinned out her once luscious hair, and made her slanted eyes void of life.

She shook her head.

Growing up with a mother like Maxine, a woman who never told her she loved her and used every chance she could to tell Miriam she never wanted her, one would think that Miriam would have written her off. But the innate desire to connect with the ones who gave you life was what seemed to have had Miriam trying time after time to gain ground with her mother. Win her over and get her to see how great of a daughter she was and that she's worthy of her love.

Nonetheless, as Miriam stared at her mother, mouth wide and reeking of gin, dozing off to sleep, she accepted that that day wouldn't bring her the peace she wanted with her mother.

As she stood and then quietly stepped out of the apartment, rather than cry when thoughts of her past with her mother came to mind, a smile lit her face thinking back to her second-grade teacher, Mrs. Rollins, who also managed to be her teacher every other year until she graduated from the eighth grade.

Knowing Miriam's home life, but seeing something inside of her, Mrs. Rollins took Miriam under her wings. Helped her to see that she was smart and valuable. It was her talks with Mrs. Rollins that helped her to stay focused in school and excel.

"Thank you, Mrs. Rollins," Miriam whispered as she descended the stairs.

4

"And now ladies and gentlemen, Deja Lafayette will perform Clair de Lune by Claude Debussy. Everyone in the auditorium clapped, especially Shawn's family, who all stood up cheering loudly as Deja took a seat on the bench in front of the upright piano. Her pale green dress draped the bench as she readied her fingers to touch the keys.

At only six years old, her minute hands tapped the keys as if she had composed the piece and had been playing it for years.

Shawn was proud of his niece, and any other time he would've been perfectly in tune with her performance, but this evening he just couldn't bring himself to focus on her in the dimly lit space. For one, he was still reeling from the fact that he had the chance to be so close to Miriam that day. She was a puzzle that he envisioned solving since the first day he laid eyes on her some ten years ago when she first started working for the company. If he hadn't been so career-driven back then, he would've pursued her. They probably would be married by now, and he would be the proud father doting on his daughter performing on stage, but instead, he decided to mark his territory with his career first. He'd hope to finally achieve something before his older brother, Chad, but things hadn't worked out that way.

Within the ten years it had taken him to get to the point he experienced in his career earlier that day in Mr. Pierce's office, his brother had become one of the top pediatric physicians in the country, had gotten married and had kids: Deja and three-year-old, Chad Jr.

If that wasn't enough to currently fray his peace, the fact that he was in competition with Miriam for the promotion did.

Trying to play catch up with his brother's accomplishments, he'd chosen to admire Miriam from afar. But that mission hadn't been easy for him either. Her brand of beauty was one he'd subscribe to any day if he could. Her dark brown hair was always smoothed back into a low bun near the nape of her neck. She was quiet mostly. Not the mean kind of quiet, the focused kind of quiet, and it intrigued him more and more over the years.

Not that he cared for the attention, but most of the

single women, and a few married ones, fawned over him and a few of the other eligible bachelors over the years. But not Miriam. She moved about her day without barely speaking to anyone other than her assistant. How reserved she was made him like her even more.

Since he never saw a ring on her finger over the years, he assumed she was neither married nor engaged. And he'd never seen or heard of any flowers being delivered to her or any fanfare sent her way during the holidays, especially not on Valentine's Day.

For him, that meant she'd been single all of that time, because the way he saw it, no man in his right mind would have a woman like Miriam and not shower her with attention, let alone gifts like bouquets of flowers delivered to her on the regular.

He relished in the opportunity of finally being so close to her earlier that day, smelling the jasmine scent of her perfume as she walked past him on their way out without so much as looking back at him.

He'd finally heard the soft melody of her voice, but the meeting with her came unexpectedly. He didn't know that the promotion he'd been working so hard to get would come at the expense of making her lose.

And unfortunately, she'd have to lose to him because as his father, Vincent Lafayette, stood hugging his brother as Deja closed out the program that night, the duo's embrace reminded him that he had no choice but to get the promotion.

"Papa." Deja ran right into her grandfather's outstretched arms as he stooped, slightly readying himself for the blow her sprint towards him would impound on his aged body.

He slobbered her with a kiss to her jaw as he stood with her in his arms. "I'm so proud of you, my Little Flower."

"You are?" She toyed with his tie as her dark brown eyes lit up, hearing her grandfather call her by his chosen name for her.

"I sure am. Just like I'm proud of the great things your father accomplishes." He patted Chad on the back.

"Thanks, Dad," Chad said, staring at the embrace between his daughter and his father.

"Shawn come over here. Why are you so far away?" Rochelle, Shawn's mother, beckoned him.

Although he'd heard their entire conversation since the show ended, he'd kept the greatest distance he could from them for the longest. He'd hoped he could avoid hearing his dad somehow manage to tie in adoration for Chad even though the spotlight should've been on Deja alone. But clearly, his father didn't know how not to do that.

Heeding his mother's request, Shawn took a slow, yet brief stroll over to his family and wedged himself between his mother and his sister-in-law, Rita.

He smiled as he watched Deja realize he was there. "Uncle Shawn, you came!" She wiggled herself free from her grandfather's embrace and ran and jumped into Shawn's arms.

He picked her up and pinched one cheek as he kissed the other. "I sure did."

She squeezed her arms again around his neck before pulling back to stare him in the face. "And did you like how I played?"

"Let me think." He put his pointer finger to his chin, and his eyes shifted from side to side as if he were searching for the answer.

She seemed to hold her breath, awaiting his response.

"Of course, I did." He smiled at her.

"I knew you would. I worked really hard on it."

"Just like your father. And that's why you're great at everything you do, Little Flower," Vincent called out to Deja.

Shawn took a deep breath as his nostrils flared.

"Is everything okay, Shawn?" his mother asked, rubbing his arm.

"Yes, ma'am. I'm just gonna go now though." He kissed Deja's cheek one more time before placing her on her feet.

"Alright bro, see you soon." Chad hugged Shawn and Vincent patted Shawn on his back.

Shawn ended the embrace with his brother and kissed his sister-in-law and mother goodbye before he made his way to the door of the auditorium.

He looked back to see the admiration in his father's eyes as he stared at Chad twirling Deja around.

Yeah, he had to get promoted to senior executive architect. Maybe then, his father would stare at him with pride the way he always managed to dote on his brother's accolades.

5

Refusing to do what he had been mulling over since he'd come to work that morning, Shawn released the doorknob to his office yet again. He laughed at himself as he returned to the seat behind his Oakwood desk.

All morning he'd been debating if he should go and say something to Miriam. It was only the day before that they had been in Mr. Pierce's office learning the conditions of his pending promotion, but he wanted to see her.

He had to see her.

She was the only thing that kept his mind free of the toil he'd experienced watching his father gloat over his brother yet again at his niece's piano recital.

He had rushed from her performance to get away from his dad and his constant adoration of his brother.

He'd pulled up the files for the Schaeffer project, but images of who he was going up against for the promotion flooded his thoughts. He abandoned getting any work done for the night and allowed himself to get lost in thoughts of Miriam. The more he tried to think of her, the more it hit him how he didn't know as much about her as he wanted to.

And that annoyed him.

All he could do was dwell on how beautiful she was. How even her modest clothing couldn't hide a body he knew had to be perfect for him. Yeah, he saw her curves under the frumpy clothes she wore. Many a time he wished he could run his hand, his tongue over them.

His fantasies didn't have much to work with, but as he made his way to his office door, he planned to commit more of her to his memory because he was certain she wasn't fleeing his thoughts anytime soon. And that was a problem for him. He couldn't have any more nonproductive nights like the one before.

In the time he'd gotten caught up thinking about her, his feet had trekked back over to his office door. He inhaled a deep breath as he held onto the doorknob yet again. "What am I worried about? I'll just go peek my head in her office, say hi, congratulate her on being up for the promotion, and then come back in here and get back to work," he mumbled, hoping his pep talk to himself would pan out the exact way he said it.

He walked down the corridor that led to her office and nodded at coworkers who walked by. He picked up speed when he walked past a few assistants huddled to one side of the hallway. They all were stealing glances at him. Some licking their lips, others pretending not to be discussing him, and one boldly winked at him.

He quickly made his way to Miriam's office and rapped on the door.

Miriam's assistant opened the door clutching a file close to her. "Mr. Lafayette, hi." She avoided making eye contact with him before she looked back at Miriam. "I'll be back in about an hour, or before if you need me." She rushed past Shawn and out to her workstation.

Shawn stood at Miriam's office door, watching her look over the papers she had sprawled out across her desk. He hoped she would invite him in.

Sensing he wouldn't leave anytime soon, she looked up at him over her black-rimmed glasses. "Yes, Mr. Lafayette, may I help you?"

Why is she being so formal with me? "Call me Shawn, please."

"Mr. Lafayette, how may I help you?"

He chuckled at her seemingly annoyance of his presence.

"For starters, can I come in?"

She pushed her glasses up on the bridge of her nose as she looked up at him. "Yes."

He inched up some and reached behind him to close

the door, but she quickly interrupted him, "No, please leave it open."

One eyebrow raised as he caught the hint of nervousness in her voice. "Okay."

There was just enough room between her office door and her desk to where she was fully able to watch his gait as he advanced towards her. She inhaled a sharp breath as an image of his bowlegs straddling her as she laid beneath him on a bed.

She took her glasses off and placed them on her desk, hoping that she could refocus her vision to see the handsome man sitting in front of her as only her competition.

She didn't know what had come over her. She hadn't envisioned herself with a man as much as she had with Shawn since they had been to Mr. Pierce's office. She'd seen him in the office for years and never gave him much thought. But to hear that deep tenor in his voice the day before, to smell his woodsy cologne, and even to see the way he had smiled at her yesterday, despite putting on her best air of indifference with him, had shifted her senses just that quick.

Meanwhile, he never thought someone could be so sexy simply taking their glasses off, but Miriam had proven to him that the unassuming act could be just that, sexy.

"Mr. Lafayette?"

"Yes?" Miriam's soft, but demanding voice had

pulled his attention from her full lips to her hazel eyes. Either focal point was a treat for him.

"How may I help you? I'm kind of busy here." She pointed to the papers on her desk.

"Yes, I see. I just came in to say congratulations to you on being up for the promotion."

"Thank you. Same to you. Is that all?" The smell of his cologne and his appraising gaze of her was overwhelming her libido.

"I, I…" He was at a loss for words at that point. Between being lost in her beautiful features, especially those cute, deep dimples in both of her cheeks, and hoping that she would've been more inviting than she was, thoughts of what he came in to say to her failed him. "I just wanted to say that even though we're up for the same position, I was hoping that we could be…friends."

"Mr. Lafayette, no offense, but if we weren't friends before now, we certainly won't be now and hereafter. You're my competition. I have one goal now, as always, to get that promotion. Nothing else."

The finality in her voice and stern look in her eyes jarred him but didn't scare him. "Okay, well I'll let you get back to your work, and I'll go get back to mine. Enjoy the rest of your day." She had said more to him within the short time that he was in her office than he had ever heard her say before.

Although his encounter with her didn't flesh out the

way he thought it would, he still came out on the winning side. He now had the sound of her voice etched in his memory.

He went back to his office with a smile plastered on his face knowing that if she ever appeared in his dreams again, as he suspected she would, the realness of her saucy voice would take center stage.

The minute Shawn closed her door, Miriam fell back in her chair, flustered. She was shocked that he came in trying to make friends with her. If she would've met him anywhere else and after her promotion, she might have been willing to welcome the idea of having a man in her life, but that wasn't the case. He was her competition. And that really annoyed her because he was so… handsome and charming.

6

"Ugh. I won't spend another Friday night in this house with you watching documentaries of people building things."

"You don't have to. You know your way around the city. Enjoy yourself." Miriam chuckled as she continued looking at her proposal on her laptop.

"No. Let's go out."

"Nope. You know my work with this proposal comes first."

"It's always work with you, Miriam. I swear you haven't dated a guy since we were in undergrad. Over ten years. Ten years." Dana held up both of her hands spread wide apart in the air to highlight the number ten. "That's too long."

"Well, we all can't have a great love like you and

Jeff did."

Dana grunted.

Miriam instantly regretted her comeback. "I'm sorry for bringing him up. I know he's still a sore spot for you."

"Not sure if you can call it great since he—"

"And don't forget about the casting call tonight for 'The Kissing Game'." The commercial on TV interrupted Dana's would've been tirade over her ex-boyfriend.

She welcomed the reprieve.

"That's it! That's what we're doing tonight." Dana jumped up from the couch, blocking a stream of sunlight coming through a window spotlighting Miriam.

"You can go, but I won't be going with you. I told you the first time we saw that commercial that I have no interest in being a part of that silly show. You know where my focus is." Miriam never looked up from her computer.

Dana rushed to Miriam and snatched her laptop from her.

"Dana, stop playing. Give it back." Miriam barked. "I didn't even press save."

"Here, I'll do it for you." Dana pressed the floppy disk icon, closed out the program and shut down the computer all the while avoiding Miriam's grasp. Out of breath, she said, "Mimi, you've been working on this day and night since you found out about it. You know how to design structures from the ground up with ease. I know this project will be no different. Girl, the promotion is already yours. I need you to live a little. Let's get out and enjoy life."

"No." Miriam brewed as she flopped back down on the couch with one leg tucked under her and her arms folded across her chest.

"Come on, Mimi. Either you'll meet the love of your life, or at the least, we'll have something to laugh about for years to come." Dana chuckled, hoping that Miriam would join in.

She never did.

"Mimi, it's one night. Just one night. I promise I won't bother you about going out again until we go out to celebrate that promotion you know you're a shoo-in to get." Dana batted her eyes rapidly, hoping to win Miriam over.

"Whatever." Miriam let out an exasperated breath as she stood from the couch and snatched her laptop from Dana's hands. She bent down to plug it up as she said, "I'll go with you, but you can't make me kiss anyone."

Dana squealed in delight. "Let's just get there for now. We'll worry about the kissing part later.

***

Miriam looked around the room and shook her

head, marveling at how many women showed up for the auditions for the silly reality show she'd been forced to attend with Dana.

"Stop doing that."

"Doing what?" Miriam turned to Dana.

"Stop shaking your head like you're not here with the rest of us." Dana laughed.

"I shouldn't be here."

"But you are, because deep down inside, you know you wanna be. You wanna see if a kiss could really seal your fate with a man."

Miriam simply stared at Dana wondering if she really was as delusional as the statement she'd just made. "No, I'm here because you held my computer hostage until I conceded to come. I knew coming would be the only way to get you off my back for the night." Miriam stared at Dana until they both broke out in laughter.

"I would think after Jeff, finding love would be the last thing on your mind." Miriam watched Dana pull in a slow, deep breath and again regretted bringing him up. "I'm sorry, Dana." She rubbed her hand and immediately thought to redirect the conversation. "What I mean is, are we really supposed to kiss a man after some of these women?" Avoiding Dana's wary eyes, Miriam scanned the large studio space filled with women from seemingly different backgrounds.

Some were dressed in goth with dark colors,

including makeup, from head to toe, while many wore tight, low cut blouses and mini-skirts that left nothing to one's imagination and a few that looked as if they put no thought into what they wore, barely matching. And there were a few others, like Miriam, that were dressed casually in semi-fitted shirts and straight-leg jeans and looked as if they too had been dragged there by their best friend, against their will.

Cameras zoomed in on women applying loads of lip gloss, touching up lipstick, staring into compact mirrors as they patted their hair, and a few of them were being interviewed by film crew while being recorded.

"Don't think about that. Just think that soon you could be having your last first kiss." Dana's eyes brightened.

Miriam donned a condescending smile as one eyebrow raised in skepticism. "Dana, this is just a reality show. I will not put anymore stake on this night than what it is, a social experiment of some sort."

"Attention, ladies. Can we have you all take a seat for a minute so that we can explain everything to you?" A preppy looking man adjusted the mic on his headset before leaning over and speaking with his assistant. He soon returned his attention to the seated participants. "Ladies, we know that the casting call didn't tell you the exact details of the night."

Some women looked to those near them and nodded their heads.

"And that was not to trick you, but we met earlier today and honestly decided to add this element to the show in Chicago."

Many eyebrows raised around the room.

He chuckled before continuing. "As you all know, you'll be filmed. We found that seeing the man or woman the person will be kissing hinders their willingness to give in to the moment, the kiss. So, with that being said, we'll blindfold you before we take you into the room."

"What?" one woman jumped up and shouted.

"Yes, you'll be blindfolded when you kiss them, but so will they. You all won't see each other until after you end the kiss. We don't want your judgment of their appearance to hinder your thoughts when kissing them. This way, you'll really get the chance to see if it's love at first kiss." He smiled, but his cheer didn't mirror the sentiment of many wrinkled-faced women in the crowd.

Some whispered their disdain as names began to be called out for the first round of kisses.

Miriam whipped her head in Dana's direction.

Dana looked down at her nails and ignored Miriam's stare.

"So, you interrupt me working on my project, bring me here to kiss God knows who, only to find out that I'll be blindfolded as well when I kiss these mysterious men?"

Dana's slim shoulders lifted slowly into a shrug as

her hands elevated in front of her. "Hey, I just found out that last bit of information the same time you did." Dana turned her head, hoping to stifle the laughter brewing in her. Miriam's annoyed look was hilarious to her.

Despite Dana not looking back at her, Miriam stared down Dana. "You owe me big time for this."

7

Dana came back into the studio space housing those waiting to be called and sat next to Miriam. She knew Miriam's arms folded across her chest, the tightness of her lips and the narrowed glare she gave her were all signs that Miriam wasn't pleased up to that point. "So, did you get called already?"

"What do you think?" Miriam asked through clenched teeth.

"I don't know, that's why I'm asking you." Dana couldn't contain her laughter. It spilled from her as she rested her head on Miriam's shoulder.

Miriam wiggled in her seat and shook Dana off her. "I don't find what I just experienced funny at all."

Dana's laughter sobered as she sat upright and positioned herself in the hard, plastic chair to face Miriam. "What happened?"

"Nothing. Absolutely nothing. No sparks. That was

the blandest kiss I've ever experienced. It was like kissing dry, unseasoned chicken."

"What?" Again, Dana worked hard to contain her laughter. If one didn't know Miriam, from the looks of her often serious demeanor, she could easily be confused with someone who lacked a sense of humor, but Dana knew better. Miriam's brand of humor was quite funny to her.

"It's not that funny." Miriam shoved Dana in the arm with her forearm.

"Yes, it is. Especially considering that's what you cooked last week. Dry and unseasoned chicken. So you know exactly how it tastes."

"Oh, hush." Miriam turned her attention from Dana as she too tried to contain her laughter.

"It's okay, you didn't have a southern grandmother like mine to teach you how to throw down in the kitchen."

Miriam got quiet thinking back to how she never knew either of her grandmothers to learn anything from them. Her mother definitely didn't care to teach her how to cook.

Wanting to escape memories that were sure to surface if she let them, she shifted her attention back to Dana. "So, how was your kiss?"

"Well, it was better than dry, unseasoned chicken but not that much better. More like broccoli with no cheese." Dana laughed at herself.

"How many more rounds of this craziness are you subjecting me to?" Miriam asked.

"I think they said like five or so, but I think that all depends on how many people connect from round to round."

"I don't think I can or want to make it through five rounds of kissing chickens," Miriam said.

"Have a little faith. Maybe this next go-round will unveil your prince."

"Miriam Caldwell."

"Or maybe another toad." Miriam huffed as she reluctantly got up from her seat and headed in the direction from which her name was called.

8

"That's it, just keep walking straight. I'll lead you right to him." Miriam's grip tightened on the assistant's lean hand, and she followed his directions on which way to walk.

Soon, his squeeze on her elbow let her know she'd made it to her designated spot. That and the strong, overbearing whiff of Old Spice seemingly coming from the guy in front of her. She was ready to run questioning what new age man sported the cologne as his scent of choice, but nonetheless, she was there and would eerily test out this round the way she did the first one.

"Damn, you smell good. I bet you look and taste good too." He made a slurping sound as he rubbed his hands together.

Although she couldn't see in front of her, Miriam's eyebrows shot up, and her head reared back as she tried to step back, but the assistant who'd escorted her in hands braced against her back and kept her from moving back further.

He leaned in and whispered to her, "Girl, just give it a try."

Still blindfolded, she turned her head in the direction she heard his voice come from and pulled on his arm as she lowered her voice. "Does he look as creepy as he's making me feel?" She held her breath, awaiting his answer.

"All I can say is give it a try." The assistant tightened his lips and pushed Miriam into the taped X she needed to stand on to fit in the camera's frame.

"Don't worry, I don't bite. That is unless you want me to." He snickered.

Miriam heard chuckling around her and was ready to turn and hightail it out of there, but Mr. Old Spice reached out and pulled her to him. "Let this game begin."

He didn't even allow her to offer up the protest her flattened palms presented his chest as he wrapped his arms around her, pulled her close to him, leaned down and immediately began sopping her up like she was warm butter and syrup spread over a biscuit fresh out of the oven.

"Hey," Miriam was barely heard as she wiggled in his arms.

Her pleas of mercy were ignored by him as his large

and heavily inflated lips made hers fully disappear when his lips even brushed against hers. But they did more than brush against hers, he inhaled her lips into his mouth and as his hands rubbed up and down her back, he pulled back from her just enough to suck on her bottom lip before inhaling them again. His full tongue traced circles around her mouth and grazed her nose as he moaned his pleasure.

"Enough!" Miriam finally garnered enough strength to push him off her and spoke loud enough for him to fully hear her. "Ugh." She snatched the blindfold off her face and blinked rapidly at the sight in front of her.

Mr. Old Spice with salt and pepper cornrows took his blindfold off and smiled wide as his front tooth gleamed from the gold cap around it. He ran his tongue across his teeth. "Just like I thought, fine." He took a step towards her, but she took a leap back.

"What? You wiggle a lot, but I thought that was you enjoying the kiss as much as I was. You know, a little cat and mouse game. I chase you with my tongue, and you pretend to run from it but know you really want it." His red eyes dropped to her feet and did a slow, thorough crawl up her body until they landed back on her lips. "You know we can get out of here right now and take this back to my place in my mother's basement. There's so much more of you I'd like to taste."

"Cut." The director no longer wanted to subject

Miriam to the man's perusal of her. Even he had become grossed out by the man in his early fifties sporting a baggy FUBU ensemble.

Mark, the director, didn't object to Miriam rushing out of the room despite Mr. Old Spice's pleas.

"Don't go, Red. I just know we'll be good together." He held his arms out as if she would come running back to them. "Don't do me like that, Red."

***

Miriam returned to the room and opted to sit away from Dana.

Dana chuckled as she grabbed her purse and rushed to occupy the empty seat next to Miriam. "I take it this round was worse than the last?"

Miriam's lips curled up and her nostrils flared as her eyes narrowed in on Dana.

"Yeah, what I just experienced was the pits too. He was so gropey. His hands were all over me." Dana scratched her arms as if she was brushing the man's hands off her.

"You're not kissing him anymore, Dana." Miriam smirked.

"I know, but that kiss was just that gross that it left an impression on me." Dana fidgeted more in her seat, trying to push the memory of the kiss out of her head.

Miriam frowned.

Dana took note of it and stopped scratching at herself. "Help me take my mind off mine by telling me how yours was."

Miriam inhaled a sharp breath and slowly let it out before she spoke, "Although I haven't kissed many, I've never known or heard of a man kissing as sloppy as the one I just experienced. Made me feel like I was a Sloppy Joe sandwich, and he was trying to catch the meat before it fell out of the bun. That was just a sloppy kiss." Miriam crossed her legs and folded her arms over her chest.

"Sloppy Joe?" Not caring about the potential stares of the women standing on the wall nearby, Dana's head bucked back as she let out a wailing laugh.

"Laugh all you want to, but I'm out of here." Miriam grabbed her purse from the empty seat to the left of her and jumped up to leave.

Dana grabbed her wrist before she could make it down the row. "Come on, Mimi. Don't go. You know they say third time's the charm."

Miriam looked back at Dana. "Yeah, and they also say three strikes and you're out, right?"

Dana acquiesced. "Yeah."

"Well, I'll be my own umpire and put myself out of this game before that third strike."

Dana laughed. "Don't go. We're here. Let's just see the night through."

With a pinched expression, Miriam looked back at

Dana.

"Dana? Dana Buchanan?" one of the assistants called out from the entrance.

"See, you have to stay. We rode together. I'm going back in which means they'll probably call you next." Dana laughed.

"Gee, lucky me." Miriam gave Dana a fake smile before flopping down in her seat.

9

It was down to the third round of hopeful matchmaking for the night.

"This must be the last round or something." Dana scanned the room with her full lips pressed into a fine line, and one of her jet-black eyebrows lifted. "It's only us and her left." Dana motioned her head towards a woman sporting a dress so tight it looked like it had been painted on her body. "Where's everyone else?" She looked to Miriam

"Either they got matched up or got smart and left, unlike us, before anymore kissing catastrophes occurred."

"Well Cruella Deville, one of us has to be optimistic, so I'll just believe that they got matched up." Dana nudged Miriam.

Miriam huffed. "I'm not Cruella Deville." She never considered herself mean, just focused. "I have hope in a lot of things, this is just not one of them."

"You just don't have hope in the good stuff, like love," Dana said.

"I do believe in love, and I'm certain I'll find it one day, but—"

"But what if it finds you first?" Dana interrupted Miriam.

"It better wait until I get this promotion at work."

Dana laughed. "It doesn't always work like that."

"It better. You know what, I'm wasting my time here. I don't have time for love or a man right now. I'm outta here." Miriam grabbed her belongings and stood.

"Miriam Caldwell?" A young man stood in the doorway of the room.

Miriam snarled as she looked back at Dana. She mumbled, "I was just about to leave."

"Maybe love says otherwise," Dana quipped as Miriam dragged her feet behind the assistant.

* * *

The assistant waved his hand and allowed her to enter the room first. Recognizing it was the same room she had two failed kisses in already that night, her jawline tensed as she gritted her teeth.

"Just put your purse and coat over there on that

chair." The assistant directed.

"Hey," she grabbed his arm and whispered to him before he walked off. "Where did all the other ladies go?"

"Honestly?" He stared at Miriam.

"Yes." She nodded.

He leaned in closer and lowered his voice. "Don't tell anyone, many of the women left after the last round, but a few of them from tonight did leave here with what looks like solid connections. Maybe this one will be yours." His blonde and thick eyebrows wriggled as he smiled at her.

Someone came behind Miriam and began connecting a microphone to her. They wanted her interaction with her kisser clearly audible.

"Okay people, come on, we need the mics ready to go and blindfolds on. Let's put them in position. We're taping here in case you all forgot. This is still a TV show," the director belted as he stood near the main cameraman.

"Say something," The man affixing the mic to Miriam instructed her.

"Something."

He laughed. "Okay, you got that?" he said into his headset to the team at the switchboards. "Okay, your audio is ready." He patted Miriam on her shoulder for good measure before walking off.

"Okay." The director looked down at the clipboard

in his hand then back up. "We'll start filming now so that we record Miriam getting blindfolded. He's being filmed getting blindfolded outside the door too. We don't want to miss a thing. Come on people. 5, 4, 3, 2, 1." He was giddy as he quietly gave cues directing the cameramen.

With a smile on his face, the assistant came back to Miriam, grabbed a blindfold from a clothing rack nearby and spun her around by her shoulders. "Relax, you should be a pro at this by now." He laughed as he secured the silk, burgundy fabric over her eyes.

Although she had been through it two times already up to that point, her familiarity with the process still didn't calm the myriad of feelings coursing through her body.

Her palms were clammy, and she wondered if it indeed would be her last first kiss, but then that thought got punted right out of her mind as the vivid images of those last two kisses she had took front and center in her thoughts. She shuttered, hating that she had to endure them and how animated they still replayed in her mind.

She set her lips to whisper a plea to the Lord about erasing the kisses from her memory for forever, but feedback in her ear reminded her that if she did say anything, it wouldn't just be between her and the Lord. Everyone else on set would hear it too. She'd talk to God later about her request, but as she felt herself being guided to a spot-on set, she knew it was best to try and focus on her then and there.

There wasn't much talking going on since the producers were eager to capture the kiss. Only after the kiss ended would the host come on set and interview the two who had been kissing.

She sensed something would be different this go-round the longer she stood there waiting for her kisser to be positioned in front of her. She was the one ushered in last her first two rounds, but this time, she had to wait for her kisser to make his grand appearance.

The waiting and her not being able to see heightened her other senses. She could clearly hear the camera tripod rolling around. She figured that meant they were moving to catch the best angles.

The door opened, and her breath seemed to catch in her throat as a scent that could only belong to a gorgeous man came closer to her.

She drew in a deep, twofold breath. On the one hand, she was trying to steady the nerves hosting the Olympics in her stomach, and on the other hand, the scent of him was familiar, but she couldn't quite figure out where she'd smelled it before.

She knew he had to be right in front of her because his earthy scent was intoxicating her in the most delightful way.

She jumped when she felt them place his hand on her arm.

His touch was electrifying, and immediately, the

space between her thighs was wet.

His big, strong hands began to squeeze her arm, trying to find a safe place to rest.

She held her breath, not knowing how much more of his touch she could endure.

She giggled as his hand teased her side, trying to find a safe space.

Reaching out to him, she touched the carefully sculpted wall that was clearly his abs. Her hand appreciatively scaled his chest until it reached his chin.

The director worked hard to contain his excitement as he witnessed the chemistry between the two. He was certain this episode would garner millions of viewers once it aired.

Further quieting himself, he looked back onto the monitor to see the man caressing Miriam's outstretched arm.

She smiled when she said, "That's my breast, not my waist. I'm clearly a lot shorter than you. Here, give me your hand." Although she hated removing his hand from any part of her body, she pulled it from her breast and their hands interlocked as she kept her other hand planted on the side of his face.

Inching on her tippy toes, she leaned into him. He was still much taller than her, so she fell into him. She found herself giggling again as his hand gripped the small of her back and pulled her closer to him.

His short breaths tickling the bridge of her nose sent

shivers down her spine. His smell engulfed her senses. Nervousness overtook her, and she giggled again.

"You nervous?" He leaned down as his lips brushed against her cheek.

She inhaled a sharp breath. "A little." Her voice was barely audible as his mere touch caressed more of her than he would ever know. It had been so long since she'd been that close to a man and enjoyed it. His touch rattled her.

"Relax, I got you." He gripped and massaged the nape of her neck as he feathered kisses on her face.

Her knees buckled and his arm around her waist tightened as he held her up and close to him.

Her feet no longer touched the floor as his lips lowered to hers. He wasn't satisfied with his lips only pressed against hers. His tongue grazed the seam of her mouth, requesting access, and when she granted it, he wasted no time in diving in.

His tongue expertly roamed her mouth as he massaged her neck and angled her head as he pleased.

She moaned from a place she didn't even know existed. Desires surfaced in her she didn't know were possible. It took every bit of resolve she had left in her not to jump up and wrap her legs around his waist. If he kissed like this, the thought of how else his tongue, his hands, his manhood, could please her gave her goosebumps.

He pulled her closer to him.

All she thought she wanted in life was to get the promotion, but this kiss she was gifted with was saying otherwise.

The way her body reacted to his touch, it was as if she needed this kiss and maybe even the kisser. Kissing him was like she was in downtown Chicago at Navy Pier experiencing the fireworks on the fourth of July. She could've sworn she heard bombs bursting in the air as she wrapped her arms around his neck and further immersed herself in his explosive kiss.

Not wanting to penetrate the force field of passion the kissers had created, but knowing they needed the host to step in, the director spoke up, giving the host her cue.

"Okay, clearly, they would go on and on and all night if we don't break them up," the stylish host said as she walked and stood next to the kissing couple. "And although we hate to stop them, we in the studio are just as curious as you all are at home to see if love at first kiss really does exist between these two."

They continued kissing, unfazed by the chatter on set.

"Folks, let me tell you all, the energy between these two right now is real. It's palpable. Almost like I can reach out and touch it. I've seen lust and I've seen love." Her small eyes widened in amazement. "I think the barometer is angling towards love for these two."

The host's words only made the man pull Miriam in closer to him as he kissed her. He'd never desired or knew it was possible to kiss a woman the way he was kissing the soft one he supported in his arms. Everything about her felt right.

He hated that their kiss would end soon, but then he'd get to see her face. And judging from the curve of her lips, the way her pert nose rubbed against his face as they kissed, and her long eyelashes fluttering against his skin, she just had to be beautiful. He couldn't imagine being disappointed by any aspect of her.

"Okay kissers, it's time to reveal yourselves to one another." The host laughed as they continued their lip-lock fest. She tapped both of them on their shoulders and yet neither pulled away from the other.

Just then a mock fire alarm rang loud in the studio and the kissers chuckled as they hesitantly began to pull away from each other, although their lips still didn't part.

He carefully put her back down on her feet and bent over, continuing to kiss her as their hands entwined with one another.

"Okay lovebirds. Let's take these blindfolds off and see what we come up with." The host stripped both of them of their blindfolds, but they each kept their eyes closed as they continued exploring each other's tastes.

"Open up your eyes and see who you've been kissing."

Miriam reluctantly opened her eyes as she drove in for one last, deep exploration of his mouth, to which he pulled her in closer to him again. His intensity matched hers, and they panted as they finally pulled apart from one another.

He smiled and licked his lips as he stared at her.

Her eyebrows furrowed, her nostrils flared, and a scowl marred her face as she stared at him. "Shawn!"

"Yes, Miriam." He smiled as he continued to hold her hands.

"What are you doing here?" she asked as her voice pitched higher than normal.

"I could ask you the same." Although he saw the scowl on her face, he couldn't hide the pleasure he'd just experienced kissing her.

Truth be told, during the kiss, the only way he imagined it would be better was if he was kissing Miriam. The woman he had been dreaming of off and on for years, but more recently chose to visit him nightly in every one of his dreams. The knowledge that he had finally tasted those big, soft, brown lips of hers left him happier than he'd been in a long time. He didn't regret their kiss, although her frown said she did.

"Wait, you two know each other?" the host, Dee Phillips, chided them.

"Unfortunately," Miriam said as she tussled to pull her hands from his and folded her arms across her plump breasts.

"Unfortunately? What's wrong with us knowing each other?" Shawn asked.

"Everything! We're coworkers, we can't kiss." Miriam grunted.

"We can, we did, and I enjoyed every moment of it." Shawn found himself licking his lips, reliving thoughts of hers pressed against them.

Miriam was certain she should still be fuming at him but to witness the act of his skilled tongue gliding across his lips, that she knew tasted good, made her forget the why. It made her want another go-round with those lips, perhaps an eternity.

Her eyes traveled up his face and locked with his. The desire in his eyes matched hers and reminded her as to why she was supposed to be angry. She scowled and continued her rant. "Why are you even here?"

"It was a last-minute thing. I saw the commercial and decided what the heck, give it a try. Why are you here, Ms. Hush? I never would've pegged you as the type to do something like this."

"You don't know me."

"But I'd like to get to know you outside of work."

"We can't."

"After a kiss like that, why not?"

Miriam's fingers touched her swollen lips as her mind replayed how his felt touching hers. He stepped forward to capture her hand as he looked into her eyes. "Miriam, there are no rules at work that say we can't date each other."

The earnest plea in his voice made her breathing stall. His endearing eyes begged of her.

She pulled her hand back from his. The currents of attraction flowing between them was too strong for her. She didn't feel in control of herself when he touched her.

"I don't care about work rules, I have my own. I have goals. I'm going to make senior executive architect, and I can't do it kissing, liking, wanting the competition." She bit her bottom lip at the last of her words before marring her face with a frown as she huffed and rushed out of the room, leaving those on set stunned with the way things turned out.

Shawn, slack-jawed, stood cemented in place.

He finally had the chance to kiss her, but it didn't end the way he thought it would.

10

Shawn walked into his two-story, brick home but didn't bother to turn on the lights. Instead, he made his way through his vestibule, took a sharp left into his den and trudged his way over to his couch and fell back, letting out a deep sigh.

He still couldn't wrap his mind around the kiss he shared with Miriam. He was certain when they were blindfolded that whoever the woman was would jump at the chance for them to be together as he would. The chemistry between them was too strong not to do so.

But Miriam thought otherwise. "I can't kiss, like, want my competition." Her last words spoken to him rang in his head.

"I saw the way she bit her lip in nervousness before she stormed out. Maybe she's just confused," Shawn mumbled to himself.

He needed to talk to someone. He needed help to make sense of what had happened. Help him to make sense of Miriam.

He wished he had a closer relationship with his brother. He knew he could be a good sounding board, but the unspoken, probably unknown wedge his father had driven between them, kept him from being close to Chad over the years. He had never talked to him about women before, so he saw no need to start then.

And as for his father, he barely said much to him outside of family functions, so he knew he couldn't depend on him to help guide his understanding of Miriam. Knowing his father, from the moment he said hello, Vincent would find a way to insert Chad into the conversation and heap praises on him.

Neither his father nor his brother could help him out, but he knew someone he hoped could.

A last resort of some sort.

Shawn was certain the conversation would be filled with just as much joking and clowning as it would be enlightening, given whose number he was dialing.

"Arty."

"Shawn, what up dawg? Shawn's co-worker and fraternity brother said into the phone.

"You busy man?"

"Not really, just pumping some iron."

"You won't believe who I kissed tonight?" Shawn

said into the phone.

"I don't wanna guess, just tell me who," Artemis said as he switched the phone from one ear to the other and continued with his bicep curls.

"Yeah, you've always sucked at playing games."

"Say that to me in the morning after I slam you on the basketball court. And who though? You didn't tell me you were going on a date when we left work. Aye, she got a friend? Hook me up with her, and we could double date tomorrow night."

"How'd you go from not guessing to concocting a whole story about a woman, her friend, and double dating?" Shawn chuckled and shook his head.

"Man, whatever. You know women are my specialty. Just tell me who."

"Miriam."

Artemis's forehead scrunched as he racked his brain. "Miriam? You said that name like I'm supposed to know who she is. But whoever she is, she sounds old with a name like Miriam." Artemis laughed at himself.

"You have the nerve to be making fun of someone's name when yours is Artemis."

"Hey, my nickname's Arty, and trust me, it sounds great when a fine honey with her legs wrapped around my waist screams it out in bed. Arty, Arty." His voice pitched higher to mimic that of a woman's voice as he panted. He laughed as he continued, "Shoot, one time I guess it got so good to a chick, she screamed out my full government name. It was like music to my ears." Artemis slowly rubbed his full and long beard.

"Shut up man. I don't wanna hear that. Miriam is not an old woman's name. Although it means rebellion or sea of bitterness, I think it's pretty on her. Meaning notwithstanding, I think it suits her just fine."

"Bruh, who is this woman that has your nose wide open knowing the meaning of her name? Why are you just now telling me how you feel about her? I thought we were boys, brothers. Why you holding out on me?" Although he knew Shawn couldn't see him, he hit his chest and shook his head, sniffling, pretending to be offended by Shawn's withholding of information.

"Dude, you know her. It's Miriam from work."

"Miriam. Miriam. Miriam?" Artemis said the name out loud trying to recall her. His eyes widened, he dropped the dumbbell from his hand and jumped up from his weight bench as it hit him exactly who Miriam was. "Miriam? Quiet Miriam at work?"

"Yup, that Miriam." Shawn smiled.

"How and where in the hell did that happen?" Artemis was fully invested in the conversation as he paced back and forth in his home gym, waiting for more details from Shawn.

"I was at home and had just settled in to watch a basketball game when I saw a commercial for auditions."

"Auditions for what?"

"Will you let me finish?"

"Okay. Aiight man, you can finish." Artemis shrugged his sculpted shoulders.

"The commercial said they were holding auditions for a show called 'The Kissing Game'."

"The Kissing Game? Like that Hi-Five song?" Artemis started humming the chorus to the 90s tune.

Shawn smiled. "I forgot about that song."

"It was the jam back then, and it's still a banger to this day, but it's that bad for you bruh that you gotta go on TV and audition just to get a kiss? You should've told me your well was dry, I could hook you up with someone in no time."

"So you can hook me up, but you're at home on a Friday night too?"

"See, I've been going on dates all week long. Tonight is like my Sabbath from women, but I'm back at it tomorrow." Artemis rubbed his beard hairs into a point as he stared at himself in the floor to ceiling mirrors in his workout room.

"Dates all week? Aren't you tired of rotating through so many women?"

"Nope. I'll chill when I come across the right one. Meanwhile, you should join the club with me. It's called single and always down to mingle."

"Nah, that life ain't for me."

"Seems like women ain't been for you the past couple of years. Not since you broke it off with Toya. I thought y'all would've made it to the altar. Married with kids by now."

"Naw, you know her and I grew apart. We accepted it and moved on." Shawn shrugged.

"Yeah, but you ain't been with nobody since her. That was three years ago, wasn't it?"

"I've dated a few here and there since then, but it seems like they were all the same type, looking for a come up. Thinking a man with a stable income will take care of them while they just shop and chill. I like a woman with drive, ambition. Willing to let me take care of her, but not afraid to get it for herself if need be. You know, go after her dreams. We should build together."

Artemis smirked. "Oh, so that's why you've been crushing on her all these years?"

Shawn's eyebrows rose in wonder. He'd never told Artemis that he was interested in Miriam.

"No need to wonder how I knew that. I peeped that a long time ago. For as many times as I've caught you staring at her as she walked by when you thought no one was looking, I saw you." Artemis laughed. "Maybe that's why it didn't work with you and Toya, she wasn't Miriam."

Shawn reclined on his sofa and propped his feet up on the ottoman in front of him.

Artemis shook his head in merriment. "Man, she has to be special. Got you knowing the meaning of her name. When did you find that out?" Artemis laughed.

"A while back." Shawn chuckled.

"From who? Because I know you didn't talk to her and held out on me with that convo too."

"Naw, I just decided to look it up one day."

"Yeah, she has your nose wide open. That kiss tonight though. Tell me how the heck that went." Artemis sat on his bench again but rolled the forty-five-pound dumbbell back and forth with his foot rather than hold it.

"So I saw the auditions and decided to go down to the studio."

Artemis chuckled.

"Laugh all you want to, but I'd do it all again given what I experienced tonight."

"I bet. So tell me about it."

"I get there and find out we'd be blindfolded during the kisses."

"They were trippin'. Ain't no way I'mma sample some merchandise before I'm able to inspect it. I always look at my food before I eat it."

Shawn shook his head at Artemis. "Miriam ain't merchandise," he said with a hint of aggravation in his voice.

"Okay, don't get testy with me. I see you've marked your territory already."

"How many more juvenile analogies are you gonna come up with?"

"Come on now, you know my wordplay is strong. I

can go on like this all night."

"Yeah, you can, just not with me. I'll end this call. Miriam is not an object."

"Clearly, but get back to your story, Mr. Sensitive."

Shawn ignored Artemis's comment. "They blindfolded us to see what type of chemistry, love as they called it, we would have together without seeing each other."

"Couldn't have been me, but was Miriam the only one you kissed?"

"Nope, I kissed two before her."

"And how were those?"

"The first was alright, I just didn't feel a connection with her. But the second one, I can't wait to get that memory out of my head."

Artemis's head fell back as he laughed. He could barely breathe as he said, "Why?"

"Why?" Shawn's voice spiked in annoyance. "Man, her lips were everywhere but on mine. She kissed my nose more than my lips."

"Naw man, it wasn't that bad."

"Yeah, it was. Felt like a dog was licking my face."

"So the third time was the charm?"

Shawn smiled. "Yep. From the moment we touched, I felt it in my bones that she would feel great in my arms. And man, when we kissed, I couldn't get enough of her."

"Was she as into it as you were?"

"Yep."

"So y'all hooking up or what?"

Shawn sighed and rubbed his face in angst. "Man, they had to literally ring an alarm to get us away from each other. That kiss was powerful."

"So again I ask, are y'all hooking up?"

"If you would've seen her face when the blindfolds came off, you'd have your answer."

"Man, quit with all the suspense and just answer the damn question. Are y'all hooking up?" He accentuated every syllable he spoke.

"She could barely breathe and steady her legs when we finally ended our kiss, but when them blindfolds came off, the way she looked at me said no."

"Maybe she was just shocked it was you, and her face wasn't telling the truth."

Shawn massaged the deep lines etched in his forehead. "Man, the way she got down on me about me being her competition for the promotion, her face and her mouth said no to there ever being more between us."

11

Miriam stepped onto her floor at work alternating between walking with her head down or scanning her surroundings to spot Shawn. At either rate, she didn't want to make eye contact with him nor speak to him. The quicker she could get to her office and lock the door behind her, the quicker she could even her breathing and get to work.

Making it into her office without any sightings of him, or anyone else for that matter, she breathed a deep and grateful sigh the minute she locked her door. Her habit of getting to work early afforded her the much-needed reprieve of avoiding him up to that point.

She rounded her desk and placed her laptop bag on it, ready to empty its contents.

Feeling a faint vibration, she took her purse off her shoulder and began rummaging through it to locate her phone. She shook her head, looking at Dana's number on the screen.

She had an inkling as to why Dana was calling her and didn't want to answer her phone for that very reason. But on the off chance that there was an emergency of some sort, either at her house or with her best friend, she answered. "Yes Dana, how may I help you?"

"You may help me by answering the questions I've been asking you all weekend."

"Well, I can't help you with that so just drop them. Just drop this inquisition of yours."

"Now, you know there is no way I can do that. You went into that last round grumpy, but you came out of it dazed, flustered, and your lips were swollen. I don't think you were grossed out by the kiss. I think you highly enjoyed it and you're holding back something from me about that kiss. I wanna know what and why?" Dana said with a playful grin on her face.

"Dana, nothing happened."

There was a knock at the door.

"I'm at work. Gotta go. Bye."

Dana could barely get a word in before Miriam hung up on her.

Another knock at her door.

"Who is it?" she called out from her seat.

No one responded to Miriam's inquiry.

Miriam began to power on her computer when there

was another knock at the door. "Who is it?"

No one answered.

She tiptoed to the door and stilled herself to hear if someone was on the other side of the door.

Not willing to open her door to see if someone was there or not, she pivoted on her heels and headed back to her desk when there was a knock at the door yet again.

She held her breath as a thought flashed across her mind. *What if it's Shawn and he knows I won't answer the door if he says his name?*

"Miriam, it's me, Camille." The mouse-like voice of her assistant made its way from the other side of the door.

With her hand over her chest, Miriam exhaled loudly before she made her way back to the door and unlocked it. When she opened it, she frowned at the petite woman. "Why didn't you say it was you the first couple of times I asked?"

"What first couple of times? I just came to your door." Camille's slender face grimaced.

I was right! Maybe it was him out there. Miriam snatched Camille into her office and peeked to see if Shawn was in the hallway. When she didn't, she quickly shut the door. Feeling relieved, she turned around to face Camille, but they crashed into one another.

Quickly trying to remedy the collision, Camille stuttered her regret. "I-I'm sorry for being so close to you, Ms. Caldwell. I was trying to see what or who you were looking for."

Miriam backed up from Camille and smoothed her blouse down. "Did you see anyone out there when you walked up?"

"No." Camille noticed Miriam toying with her glasses. "Are you okay?"

"I'm fine. Just fine." Miriam's voice reflected a hint of snip in it. "What did you come in here for?" she asked, massaging her temples with her back to Camille. She really was on edge.

"Ms. Caldwell, I come in here every morning to recap what we did the day before and preview what we need to accomplish for the day." Camille kept her head down, hoping she hadn't crossed the line with her boss.

"Oh, you're right." Miriam braced herself on her desk and took slow, steady breaths. She turned to face Camille again. "I'm sorry for being so snippy. I just, I…can you give me some time alone? I'll email you what I need you to do and call you back in here if I need anything else."

"Okay." Camille nodded, placed the folders she had in her hand on Miriam's desk and then left the office.

Miriam was on Camille's heels making sure she closed and locked the door the moment Camille stepped out.

Her shoulders slumped as her head tilted back against the door.

She clenched her thighs tight together, realizing she needed to use the bathroom, but she would much rather see how long she could hold it than chance seeing Shawn in the hallway.

***

Shawn sat at his desk, drumming his pencil on the blank sheet of paper in front of him. Although much of what he did for his projects could be done using a computer, he still preferred the old-school way of putting pencil to paper at times. He first fleshed out his ideas in pencil and transferred them onto the computer software either before he left work or when he got home.

While he saw the benefits of using the computer software, pen and paper just felt right to him, like the kiss he shared with Miriam.

He'd been thinking about her ever since the kiss Friday night.

Every time he sat down with pencil in hand and paper on his lap, the vivid vision of holding her supple body close to his as he explored her mouth hindered his ability to focus on anything but his thoughts of her. He couldn't forget the sound of her moans humming in his mouth. The feel of her fingers caressing his head as they kissed still wowed him. Her taste still lingered on his tongue.

It was like before the kiss, she frequented his fantasies ever so often, but now that he actually knew what it was like to kiss her, hold her, hear her voice so intimately in his ear, she was no longer a fantasy but a reality he wanted to live daily.

Being accustomed to her consuming his thoughts since they were in Mr. Pierce's office, he dismissed the thought of getting any work done as he sat back in his tufted leather swivel chair and gave in to his imagination.

He never would've pegged her as the type to even do a show like that. Hell, he didn't even know why he was at the audition. Outside of his trek to the top in the silent competition with his brother, he really was an adventurous person. But her, she was always focused at work, which made him believe she was that way outside of work.

Let any of her coworkers tell it, she was stuffy. He would've never imagined her going to that audition to kiss complete strangers. Truth be told, many of her coworkers assumed she didn't even like men. No one had ever seen or heard of her with a man or any partner for that matter.

He was glad that she was apparently single and had gone to the audition because it gave him the chance to connect with her through their kiss. "Yeah, that definitely was more than a kiss," he said out loud as he nodded his head and placed his steepled hands under his chin.

He rested his elbows on the arms of his chair as he continued to think about her. He just couldn't get her soft lips and perfect body out of his mind. But he knew he had to.

The only way he would become S.E.A. was if he buckled down and focused on creating the best proposal for the hotel to win over its owner and his boss.

"Maybe if I find out a bit more about her, it would satisfy my curiosity enough to get back to my work until this promotion is over with. Then I'll really pursue her." Shawn straightened the tie around his neck, reveling in what he thought was a genius solution to his lack of focus.

He opened his door and scanned the cubicles ahead of him and the long corridors stretching out to the left and right. Just then, Artemis walked up to him. "What are you doing just standing there looking like that?" Artemis tossed a red apple up in the air before he took a big bite out of it.

"Like what?" Shawn hadn't made eye contact with his friend as he continued his stationary search for someone who might know more info about Miriam.

"Like you've got an idea but don't know how to execute it."

"What?" Thick, jet black eyebrows raised in query. Shawn finally looked at Artemis.

"I'm saying, you're normally so calculated and

smooth with everything you do. But right now, you looked stumped. Constipated." Artemis laughed as he took another bite out of his snack.

Shawn stared Artemis up and down as if questioning what planet he came from. "You can go back the same way you came from with that."

Artemis laughed and shoved Shawn in the shoulder. "I'm just saying, you need to get it together. Stand here any seconds longer with that look on your face, dufus, and somebody might think—"

Shawn quickly snatched Artemis by his arm into his office and closed the door.

"Hey, why so hostile?" Artemis asked as he straightened his shirt. "And you could've made me choke on my apple." Artemis looked down at his apple. No longer wanting it, he threw it into the garbage near the desk and grabbed hand sanitizer to remove the stickiness from them.

He studied Shawn leaning against a chair with his hands in his pockets. He still wore a pensive look which made Artemis further question him. "What is up with you, man?"

"I was looking to see if I could spot anyone on the floor who might know something about her." Shawn braced his hands on the back of the chair.

"Her who?" Flustered with confusion, Artemis's face reddened.

"You know who. Miriam."

Artemis shook his head at Shawn. "So, you're willing to put your cool reputation on the line by standing in the hallway looking like a creep?" He shook his head before rounding the chair near him and sitting in it.

"I wasn't looking like a creep. But for real, who do you think might know info about her?"

"You ever thought about just asking her what you want to know about her? Duh. That's a no brainer. Clearly, you'd be lost without me." Artemis relaxed in his chair and folded one leg over the other, exposing his eclectic sock collection.

Again, Shawn looked at Artemis from head to toe. "Why am I even talking to you? A man who thinks it makes sense to mix several colors and varying patterns all in one outfit." Shawn scanned Artemis from head to toe, taking note of his vibrant, multi-colored striped socks; his gray, subtle pinstripe pants; his lavender dress shirt; and an argyle tie mixed with varying shades of purple, blue, and gray.

Artemis stood up, smoothed out his slacks and straightened his tie before he walked over to Shawn. He pointed a strong honey almond-colored finger at him. "You talk to me because I make sense and haven't steered you wrong yet."

Shawn guffawed.

"I'll ignore that." Artemis smirked. "Why won't you just talk to her? You never know, she may have had time to get over the shock of kissing a coworker and have realized that she likes you too."

Shawn's eyes brightened with the hope of Artemis's scenario being accurate. "Hold on a second." A shapely figure passing by the frosted sliver of glass next to his office door caught his attention. He darted out of his office. He was right. It was Miriam he saw, and she was heading towards her door.

He quickened his steps as he called out her name, "Miriam."

She looked back at him with wide eyes filled with nervousness. Tongue-tied, she rushed to her office and locked the door behind her.

Eyes were trained on Shawn as he hurried his steps to her door. Taking deep breaths, he knocked on it. "Miriam, it's Shawn."

A coworker walked by, and he merely nodded at the woman who he knew to be the office gossip. He didn't want her privy to anything he might say to Miriam.

What was he going to say to her?

There was silence on the other side of the door, but he knew she was in there. He'd just saw her walk in, and like his office, hers only had one door to enter and exit from.

He leaned in closer and spoke loud enough to hopefully just be heard by her. "Miriam, it's me, Shawn. Can we talk for a second? You know, about Friday night." He stood with his ear pressed to her door for about two minutes before he surmised she wouldn't open it.

He walked back to his office and closed the door. Bummed, he walked over to his plush, high back executive chair and sat in it.

All the while, Artemis stood nearby. He noted Shawn's dazed look. "Yo, where'd you go?"

Shawn looked up at him." Oh, I forgot you were still in here." His face relaxed into a frown.

"You told me to hold on. What's up?"

"I took your advice and decided to go say something to her."

"So, how'd it go?" Artemis pulled up the chair behind him and stared at Shawn.

"She didn't open her office door."

"Well, how'd you know she was in there?"

"Because when I saw her heading to it, I called her name. She looked back at me, almost like she was shocked to see me, and then rushed in her office and locked herself in there."

Artemis pinched his lips together, trying to keep from laughing, but Shawn could tell he thought what he'd said was funny. Artemis's body noticeably jerked as he tried to hold in his laughter.

Shawn splayed his hand towards him. "Just let it out. No sense of holding it in."

Artemis's mouth flew open, and out came an

uproarious laugh.

Shawn simply stared at him. "You done now?"

"I think." Artemis continued laughing himself into a choking fit. Once he cleared his throat, he looked back at Shawn. "Okay, I'm done now."

"You sure? Even though I don't find anything funny."

"I know. From your view, I'm certain it's not funny. But from my angle, it's hilarious. I'm looking at a man who's been low-key pining after a woman for years, by some strange happenstance, shares a passionate kiss with her, as you say, and now it seems she's avoiding you. This is the type of stuff the mushy romance books and movies are made of." Artemis's smile stretched from ear to ear as he tried to quell his laughter again.

"You done?" Shawn raised one eyebrow at Artemis.

"Yes, no more laughing at your dilemma. For now." He mock-coughed out the last of his statement.

Shawn shook his head at Artemis's amusement of his situation.

"I can understand you wanting to talk to her, make some sense of the kiss, see if there could be more between you two, but why were you trying to get info on her from others?"

Shawn sat back in his chair again and folded his arms behind his head. "I don't know, see if someone could tell me some things I don't know about her so I could know how to step to her."

"Try her assistant," Artemis blurted out as he stood and began rotating his body as he practiced his golf swing.

"I don't know. After Miriam just gave me the cold shoulder, talking to her assistant might make things worse."

12

By lunch, Shawn had enough of failing at trying to work on his project. He needed to know more about Miriam, and with her avoiding him, he'd have to get his answers from someone other than her. He shook his head, admitting that Artemis was right. If he couldn't get his info straight from the source, then her assistant just might be the next best option.

He stood from his desk and stretched his long, muscular limbs high and wide. His stomach growled, and he reasoned he might as well grab lunch from one of the food trucks parked outside the building.

He grabbed his blue suit jacket and went in search of Camille.

Walking down Miriam's corridor, he spotted Camille talking to another assistant at the end of the hallway. The closer he got to her, the more he questioned whether or not she would actually help him.

She was quiet herself, just like Miriam. If it weren't for her being so mousy, he might have likened her to Miriam, but he knew he couldn't do that. Without knowing much personal info on either of the women, it was clear to see that Miriam had a quiet strength, a commanding authority about her.

His steps drew closer to Camille, who seemed to be averting eye contact with him when he spotted Miriam out of the corner of his right eye. She was in the break room, refilling her coffee mug.

He was at an impasse, either he could corner her and force her to speak to him or carry on with his original plan and talk to Camille.

He peeked in the break room to see other coworkers in a huddle talking and figured that Miriam would feel some type of way about him if he approached her with others around. Refusing to speak to her didn't stop him from staring at her.

As usual, she had her hair in the low bun near the nape of her neck and had on her wire-rimmed glasses, sitting almost on the tip of her nose. He found the act of her frequently pushing them up oddly alluring to him. Her pants nor her top flattered her, but thanks to their kiss, her closeness to him days before, he knew just how soft her body was. The curve of her hips. The dip in her lower back. That knowledge had him smirking as he stared at her.

"Shawn, come in here for a second." One of his coworkers spotted him as he stood in the doorway.

Miriam looked up, red and seemingly annoyed with his presence. She turned her back to him as she stirred the creamer in her coffee.

"I'll catch up with you all later." He nodded at his coworkers and glanced one last time in Miriam's direction before resuming his steps toward Camille.

When Miriam finally felt it was safe to flee from the break room and back to the sanctuary that was her office, she peeked her head out of the breakroom only to see Shawn down the hallway engrossed in a conversation with Camille. One eyebrow raised. "What business does he have with her?" she mumbled to herself as she sprinted across the hall to her office.

***

Miriam stormed into her condo and shoved her door closed. Her lips were drawn tight, and she looked tense as she rushed past the big screen TV and headed to her bedroom, slamming the door behind her.

"Hello to you, too." Dana sat up on the couch with one brow arched high in Miriam's direction. She threw the covers off her and shuffled to Miriam's bedroom. She rapped twice on the door. "Mimi, what's wrong?" She didn't hear Miriam respond but she gathered she was upset from the sound of things hitting the floor. "I'll set dinner out, and we can talk over food, water, and wine."

Dana headed to the kitchen and began warming up the contents of Tupperware from Sunday's dinner.

When she knew the pasta and pan-seared chicken was piping hot, she put portions of each on two plates and put them on the dining table. She went back and grabbed a bottle of red wine situated in a rack near the kitchen sink. She grabbed her goblet and placed it on the table right when Miriam flopped into an empty chair at the table.

Dana sat down opposite of her. "What is wrong with you?" She stared at Miriam with her elbows propped on the table and her fork swirling in her pasta.

"I don't wanna talk about it." Miriam frowned.

"Mimi, please stop acting like I won't hound you until you fess up. You've been in this funky, neurotic mood since Friday night. Dish. And I do mean now."

Miriam grunted knowing that Dana would indeed hound her until she learned of what happened with that last kiss Friday night. She let out a long sigh before she pushed her plate aside and gobbled down all the water in her glass.

Dana's lips pinched together as her eyes widened. "That must've been one heck of a kiss. I know you don't drink alcohol, but with the way you finished that water, you sure you don't want just a little sip of wine to knock that edge off you?"

"No." Miriam stared hard at Dana.

Dana held up her hands in surrender.

"Are you gonna let me talk or what?" Miriam sneered at Dana.

Dana fell back into her chair, pretending to zip her lips and throw away the key.

"I kissed Shawn Friday night."

Again, Dana's brow rose in curiosity. "Who is Shawn, and why was kissing him so bad for you?"

Miriam stared at Dana with wide eyes as if she shouldn't have to explain much about her dilemma, she should just magically know. "Shawn is my co-worker."

"So what. People date their coworkers all of the time."

"Shawn is the one I'm in competition with for the promotion."

"Oh, I can see how that might present a conflict of interest for you. But if you play your cards right, you can seduce your way into him conceding the promotion over to you." Dana smiled, believing she'd just given the perfect solution to what Miriam considered a problem.

Miriam stared incredulously at Dana. "Why are we best friends if you don't even know me? Me seduce a man to get what I want? Me be okay with getting a promotion based on lust, sex, trickery instead of earning it myself? You must not know me at all." Miriam backed away from the table and headed to her living room.

"Oh, so we need a trek back down memory lane of our beginnings?" Dana grabbed her plate and wine from the table and followed her.

Once in the living room, she placed her food and wine on the coffee table and then sat Indian style on the couch catty-corner from where Miriam sat.

"No." Miriam shook her head and waved her hands at Dana.

"Nah, you asked, so I'll answer. Let's see."

Miriam dropped her head in her palm as she prepped herself for Dana's retelling of how they met.

"It was our freshman year of college. You at Cornell and I was at NYU Tisch School of the Arts."

"As if I didn't know that." Miriam rolled her eyes.

"Whatever. I'm proud of my alma mater, and I know you're proud of yours."

Miriam smiled at the truth.

"Any who, you didn't want to return home to your mother your first winter break away, so you came up to New York for the weekend."

"Our beginning. Yes, short and sweet." Miriam clapped her hands and lifted from the couch.

Dana threw her forearm out to stop Miriam from moving off the couch. "Unh unh, you gotta sit through this whole reminder." Dana chuckled as she took a sip of her sweet wine.

Miriam grunted as she sat back down.

"Picture it, New York, 2004—"

"You've been watching too much Golden Girls, starting your story off the way the mother on there does."

"Estelle Getty is goals." Dana laughed. "As I was saying, the year was 2004, a quiet, yet inquisitive Miriam Caldwell wanting to branch out and possibly meet some new people, stumbled across a low attendance frat party.

"Girl, you came in with that banging body of yours and had most of the fellas checking you out whether their girls were there or not. Except for my man. He only had eyes for me."

"You love overexaggerating so much of this story when you retell it, except for Jeffrey. He couldn't take his eyes off you if someone held a gun to his head and demanded that he look away."

"Yeah, well he eventually looked away from me, but that's beside the point. Most of the guys in there were checking you out, but they all fell back when the captain of all captains, Dorian, staked his claim on you."

Miriam shook her head and huffed, knowing there was no use in trying to shut Dana up at that point.

"Y'all was over on that couch chatting away so much that the man had given you a nickname within the first three minutes of talking to you. 'Mimi'." Dana swooned the last of her words. "Girl, he was so into you.

I was talking to pledge Jeffrey and I overheard the hater, which you know can be difficult for me at times, even with my hearing aids volume up high. But I heard her. The jealous heffa was taking jabs at you."

"I didn't hear her."

"I know. You only had eyes and ears for Dorian."

Miriam rolled her eyes, flashbacking to her brief infatuation for Dorian.

"With how much your nickname rolled off his tongue, the way he played with your hair, your bright tail couldn't hide those blushing red cheeks of yours. And with that insanely bright smile you had on your face, anyone could see how hard you and Dorian were hitting it off."

"Dana, I was there. You can end the story now."

"Nope, I've started. I might as well finish it. Even if we're the only ones here and we know it." She laughed and took a quick sip of her wine. "Stop interrupting me." She smirked. "Like I was saying, that jealous heffa was hatin' on the attention Dorian was showering you with and started mockingly calling you Mimi and saying childish stuff about you. She was loud with her chiding and soon her three little ratchet friends joined in trying to clown you.

"I could tell they thought you were a punk with how quiet you were, aside from you chatting with Dorian. Truth be told, with the way you moved through the house and barely made eye contact with people before

Dorian cornered you, I could tell you were out of your element. A shy girl, but I wasn't going to confirm that with them.

"Quick on my feet, I called your nickname and carried on the conversation with you like you were my cousin. Which by the way, you do act like my shy cousin Tia from the Delta at times."

Miriam laughed. "Whatever. There's nothing wrong with Tia. We just keep to ourselves most often. And Dana, end this story already."

"Almost there. Would've been done with it if you wouldn't keep interrupting me."

Miriam side-eyed Dana.

"Like I was saying, them heffas thought they were about to clown my new cousin, so I squashed it."

"You didn't know if I could fight or not, it might have got down to you against the four of them. How were you going to handle them?"

"Child, bye. Everybody there knew I was Jeffrey's girl so his line brothers and their girls, who I was cool with, were not going to let anything happen to either you or me. But I explained that to you that night."

"I know, but if you're acting like I wasn't there when all of this went down, I might as well play along and ask questions." Miriam laughed.

"Whatever. That whole retelling was necessary to remind you that we've been tight ever since that night. You got a nickname that night, and I got my friend for life. So yes, I *am* your best friend.

"We've been through so much together over the years. I know you're not scandalous and deceitful so I was joking with saying you could play him to give you the promotion. But I'm serious when I say I think this Shawn, this man who has your feathers all ruffled, panties in a bunch, is good for you. He's made you come alive. You showed more emotion leaving the studio Friday night and just now than you have since that first time I met you. Besides, who said there's anything wrong with you dating a coworker?"

"Me!" Miriam pointed to herself.

"Why?"

"Because, I believe work romances mess up productivity at work. Those involved get too busy playing kissy face and doting on one another that their work performance often suffers. And what happens when the romance doesn't work out? That spells awkwardness and drama at work. All of which you know I love to avoid."

"Yes, those are the negative possibilities, but I need you to focus on the positives."

"There aren't any." Brooding, Miriam sat back on the couch with her arms folded.

"Yes, there are." Dana found herself smirking as she sipped her wine.

After waiting for an extended period of time for Dana to highlight the positives, Miriam finally looked to see Dana staring at her. "Why are you smiling like that?"

"Because, you obviously like him and that kiss had to be amazing if he, it, has you all worked up as you are. Come on Mimi, tell me about it. The kisses I experienced were awful. At least I can experience some type of bliss through yours."

Miriam shook her head. "You can't." She found herself slowly running the pad of her thumb across her lips as her mind recounted Shawn's full lips pressed against hers. She'd never known she could experience such pleasure from just a kiss.

Dana's laughter pulled Miriam out of her reverie.

"What's funny?"

"I know that look."

"What look?" Miriam wedged a pillow between her chest and lap and drew her knees closer to her chest.

Dana finished chewing her bread before she continued. "I caught that far off look in your eyes and the way you rubbed your fingers across your lips. Still feel that kiss, hunh?"

Miriam pursed her lips. "No."

"You're not fooling me. I had enough of those kisses with..." Dana harrumphed, refusing to mention his name. She snatched her goblet off the table and gulped a mouthful of wine. "Okay, I'm back."

"Dana, it hasn't been that long since you two broke up. You don't talk about it, about him. You need to. I'm here for you when you're ready." Miriam angled her body towards her friend.

"The same way you need to open up to me about your kiss with this Shawn guy? Your attraction to him."

Miriam grabbed the pillow on her lap, covered her reddened face with it and screamed into it. She finally took it off her face. "Ugh!"

"You done now?" Dana's intense stare forged the words from Miriam's mouth.

"Okay. The kiss was amazing. Kissing Shawn was amazing. I didn't know kisses like that were possible." Miriam's smile grew wider as her mind recalled Shawn's hands squeezing her.

Dana squealed, watching her best friend come to life. "Yes, that's it. Feel it. Feel something. Open yourself up."

Dana's words marred Miriam's face with a frown. "I can't."

"Oh, why the heck not?" Dana threw her long limbs up in the air.

Miriam jumped up from her seat and paced the floor near the couches. "Because, that's not my thing. Guys have never been my focus. Architecture and design have always been my thing, my treasures. You know that."

"But you can have both, Mimi." Dana's loud voice held desperation in it.

"No, I can't. I *need* to reach my career goals before

I entertain the idea of adding a man to the mix." Miriam stopped pacing the floor for a second and turned a stern stare to Dana. Her light brown eyes danced with determination. "And when, and if, I do add a man to the mix, it certainly won't be the likes of Shawn Lafayette."

"Why not? What do you know about him that's a turnoff? Although that kiss you two shared suggests you're into him," Dana mumbled the last of her words.

Miriam gave her an "I heard that" look before saying, "He's just not my type. He's a ladies man."

"And how do you know that?"

"I just do. I've seen so many women around the office swoon over him over the years."

"So he's dated a lot of them?"

"No, I mean, I don't know." Pouting, Miriam ambled her way back over to the couch she vacated moments earlier and flopped down on it.

"Have you ever talked to him?"

"Nope. Mr. Pierce introducing us to one another was the first time I'd actually spoken to him."

Dana neared the end of the couch and clasped her hands together as she stared at Miriam. "So, let me get this straight, you don't really know him, other than he's an amazing kisser and can make your toes curl."

"Hey, I didn't say that." Miriam's eyes widened.

"Stay focused here while I break this down. You know he's an amazing kisser, and you don't have any evidence that he's a ladies man. He's gainfully employed, educated, ambitious since y'all are going for the same spot, and yet he's not your type? What is your type then?" Dana cocked her head to the side.

"Oh, shut up. I just know it's not him. He can't be. He's my coworker and you wouldn't believe that I caught him in the hallway talking to Camille at work today."

"You don't say." Dana feigned being shocked.

Miriam sneered at her. "Later on, Camille came in all hushed to tell me that Shawn had asked her about me."

"Well, what did he ask, and what did she tell?"

Miriam pursed her lips and sighed. "My likes and dislikes. He said he didn't know anything about me because I always kept to myself around the office over the years. He wanted to know more about me to get a better read on me."

Dana perked up. "I like this Shawn. And I told you you needed to be more social at work. Stop being such a hermit."

"Nothing is wrong with the way I am."

"I'm not saying it is. And because you're so great, that's even more reason to share yourself with others. Especially Shawn." Dana wiggled her eyebrows as a smile danced across her face.

"Whatever. I'm just glad that Camille didn't betray me and tell him anything about me."

"I'm not. I think this Shawn will be good for you."

"What's good for me is getting this promotion. Yep, I just need to hurry up and get this promotion, then I'll be good. All will be well with me." Miriam grew eerily silent, and Dana knew exactly why.

Dana was hesitant to speak up about the matter because she knew how touchy of a subject it was for Miriam, but she desperately wanted her friend to get beyond the pain of her past, move forward and live life on her own terms. "Mimi, you can't keep living your life trying to prove yourself to her," she whispered her words, but the mist in Miriam's eyes let her know Miriam had heard what she said.

She didn't want Miriam to keep opening old wounds, but maybe this time, maybe with this talk, Miriam would peel the bandage completely off. Air it out so the wound could heal properly. "With what you've already accomplished in your life, you've more than proven yourself to her if that's what your goal still is."

"You don't get to determine that for me. I do." Miriam's voice cracked.

"I know I don't Mimi, I'm just saying that what you've accomplished already is book-worthy. Live for you, not to prove something to her." Dana hoped the sincerity in her voice would reach out to Miriam and finally push her past the mentality that seemed to stifle the cheerful glow she knew was burning deep inside of her. But after double digits of years of friendship, she knew Miriam's tight lips and squared shoulders meant she hadn't gotten through to her.

"I am living my life on my own terms," Miriam blurted as she sprang up from the couch. "This promotion will not only prove to me, but to her, that I was worth being born. How great of a person I am." Tears clouded her vision as she headed to her room, but Dana's firm grip on her wrist stopped her from leaving the living room.

Dana stood from the couch to be eye level with Miriam. "I'm sorry, I won't bring her up again."

"It's okay." Miriam inhaled a deep breath and willed her tears away before they spilled from her eyelids.

"But we can get back to talking about Shawn." A sly smile crept on Dana's face. "You haven't described to me how he looks." Dana pulled Miriam down on the couch with her.

Miriam shook her head as she settled next to Dana.

"How tall is he? Low cut? Waves? Slim? Lots of muscles or little muscles?" Staring at Miriam, Dana folded her long legs under her as she eagerly waited for her questions to be answered.

Miriam dropped her head in her palms and silently cursed herself for letting her best friend move in with her. Because at the moment she wished she didn't have Dana there forcing her to talk about Shawn. "So what he's about 6'3, built like he uses a sledgehammer like a house hammer and could easily do hundreds of pull-ups on a high beam. Deep and dark yet also light brown, soul-searching eyes. Perfect teeth like both of his parents are dentists, and he smells like a beautiful day by the ocean. Firm lips but still soft like my favorite pillow, and tastes like the man of my dreams.

"But none of that matters. If, when, I get this promotion, it'll put me on a different floor from him and then hopefully, I'll never have to see him again. Goodnight." Miriam got up from the couch and headed to her room.

"I think you being his boss would cancel out never seeing him again. And you're leaving me hanging after that mouthwatering description of him?" She looked at the bold numbers on her phone screen not too far from her. "It's only eight o'clock at night," Dana said, annoyed that Miriam had called it a night.

Miriam closed her bedroom door and trudged over to her bed. She pushed her mother to the back of her mind the best she could, leaving her with the vivid memories of her kiss with Shawn. Thoughts of him refused to cease or at least lay dormant.

"I know what time it is," she mumbled, thinking about Dana pointing at how early she turned in for bed. "If he's gonna visit my dreams the way he did over the weekend and interrupt my sleep, I need to get a head start on trying to get some shut-eye." She turned her night light off and fell face-first onto her bed.

13

Miriam showed up for work the next morning all out of sorts. With the things Shawn did to her in her dreams, she kept forcing herself to wake up all throughout the night to stop his hands, his tongue, his essence from roaming all over her. But no matter how many times she fell into the pattern of waking up and rolling over, the minute she closed her eyes, there he was again in her dreams. Vividly teasing and pleasing her.

If it were any other man invading her thoughts like that, maybe she could've given in to the erotic scenes unfolding in her psyche, but because it was Shawn, she had to cast down her imaginations.

And boy were they vivid.

It was almost as if she felt his big hands touching her all through the night. And even as she stood at the coffee machine in the breakroom, she could feel the weight of his hand on her shoulder, smell his soft, woodsy-amber and gauzy-musk cologne. She could hear him breathing in her ear.

She slowly licked her lips thinking that maybe, just maybe, if she gave in and let the scene unfolding in her mind fully play out that she could dismiss it.

She heard him calling her name. God, it sounded so good rolling off his tongue. She moaned low as his scent filled her nose and he said her name again, "Miriam."

Oh, what the heck. "Shawn." She moaned his name as her eyes closed and her head fell back into something. She didn't know what it was, and quite frankly, she didn't care. All she knew was that she was in tune with the way he was saying her name as his hands craftily roamed her body.

"Miriam, your cup is overflowing."

She quickly opened her eyes and turned to her left to see Shawn staring at her with one raised brow.

Looking past him and slowly scanning her surroundings, it hit her that she wasn't lying in bed with him as her imagination had suggested moments earlier, but that she was in the breakroom at work.

She quickly snatched her overflowing mug from the machine and raced out the door ignoring Shawn's pleas for her to come back.

She slammed and locked her office door, took her seat, and begin to bang her head on her forearm resting on her desk.

She took a deep breath and then sat up. "Okay, you cannot let that happen ever again." She shook her head at herself. *See, that's a perfect example of why I can't be involved in a work romance, they can make for really awkward moments.*

Her hand flew up to cover her gaping mouth. *Did he hear me moan his name?*

"Oh, my God. I can't believe this." She buried her face in her hands. "I should just go home for the rest of the day and work from there. Maybe even until this whole promotion process is over."

Just then there was a knock at the door. She stilled herself and paused her breathing.

The knocking continued.

What if it's him coming to discuss what he just heard? She could no longer hold her breath, but too afraid to make even the slightest sound and alert him of her presence in her office, she let out a quick breath, but instantly inhaled another to continue holding her breath.

"Miriam, it's me, Camille. Will you let me in?" Miriam let out an audible sigh of relief as she raced from behind her desk and inched her door open. She peeked through the crevice and stared at Camille's raised eyebrows.

"Can I come in or should I come back later?" Camille murmured.

Miriam opened the door enough to poke her head out and checked to see if she would spot Shawn.

Camille's small eyes followed Miriam's paths of vision too. "Is there something I should know?"

Miriam looked back at Camille as if her behavior was normal and shouldn't be questioned. "Just come in and lock the door behind you." Miriam turned and walked back to her desk and stood in front of it.

Camille did as instructed and stood with a file folder clasped in her hand and at an arm's length in front of Miriam. She kept her lips tight as she stared at Miriam.

"Oh, don't look at me like that." Miriam folded her arms over her chest and leaned back against her desk. "Shawn may or may not have heard me say some things in the breakroom."

"Who were you talking to? What did you say?"

Miriam couldn't help but notice the tempered excitement in Camille's voice. She was doing a poor job of keeping a straight face too.

"I wasn't talking to anyone and it doesn't matter what I said," Miriam's words faded out.

"So why worry if he was at your door?"

Miriam looked at Camille the same way she looked at Dana when explaining the kiss to her, in astonishment.

Why couldn't they see that Shawn was a problem for her?

"Because, after the stuff you told me he asked about me, I don't know if he was just coming to be straight forward with me." Flustered and red, Miriam rounded her desk and sat down. The day had barely started, and she was already drained.

"Well, if I may speak up on the matter, Ms. Caldwell?" Camille fidgeted with the folder in her hand.

"You know you can call me Miriam, we're pretty much the same age. I'm not your elder." She peered over her glasses and stared at her petite assistant.

"Well, Miriam, I think it's great that Mr. Lafayette is interested in you. I've been your assistant for three years and not once have I heard you talk about a man. At all."

"There's nothing wrong with that," Miriam snipped.

Camille was nervous that she may have gotten ahead of herself given Miriam's narrow stare at her. She raised her hands in defense as she said, "I'm not saying it is, I'm just saying, with as pretty as you are, I'm just surprised that you don't get offers for dates from the guys around here all of the time.

"I'm surprised you aren't taken by now." She lowered her head after watching Miriam push her glasses up on the bridge of her nose. That generally meant the wearer was about to tell someone off. She hoped not to be on the receiving end of a tongue lashing for her observations of her boss.

A faint smile graced Miriam's face. Her normally mousy assistant was being more vocal than she ever had been, but Camille being quiet never bothered her because she was reserved as well. "Thank you for the compliment. You sound like Dana, but you should know by now that my main and only concern is my career goal of getting this promotion."

Camille merely nodded her head. She didn't want to say any more and actually cross the line with her boss.

Miriam would've continued explaining herself, but she looked down at her watch and realized how much time she'd wasted that morning centered on Shawn.

She already struggled with getting there as early as she normally did because of Dana. Her best friend had asked to use her car that morning to go to a dance audition in a northern suburb of Chicago, yet Miriam had to force her to wake up and get ready to leave out so that she could get her to work on time.

Miriam knew she needed to get down to business and hopefully what Camille was clutching to her chest in the manila folder would be exactly what she needed to refocus. "Is that for me?" She reached out for the folder.

Camille handed it to Miriam. "Yes, but—"

Miriam scanned the contents. "But...this is not what I was expecting." She continued searching the documents in the folder for the additional blueprints she needed to add the specs to her presentation she knew would help her win the promotion. "But what?" She looked up at Camille, seeking an answer to the question she didn't even have to utter.

"But Mr. Schaeffer sent over enlarged versions of everything you need."

"Okay, bring them in and I'll spread them out over there." She pointed to her workspace to the right of her office door. She walked to it and began clearing it off.

Realizing that Camille wasn't gone yet, Miriam looked over her shoulder to see Camille was still where she left her in front of her desk. "Camille, will you go get them for me, please?"

Camille hesitantly began to speak as she turned to face Miriam, "Here's the thing, I know you like to work by yourself in your office, but when told by Mr. Pierce's assistant where the blueprints were, he said that Mr. Pierce specifically said to leave them in the Skylight Conference Room.

"What? But Mr. Pierce knows I need them to finish my proposal." Miriam's forehead wrinkled.

"I know, but the documents have to remain in that conference room as he said. Sorry."

"Ugh! That means I'll have to work in there for a couple of days."

Miriam turned a shade of red Camille had never quite seen on a human before.

Miriam paced the floor for a second but stopped abruptly and turned to face Camille. "How about we make copies of the blueprints and then I can still work in here?" Miriam stared at Camille's pensive expression. "Why are you looking like that wasn't a good idea?"

"It would be a great idea if it were allowed, however, Mr. Pierce said no copies can be made. That one and only set has to remain in the Skylight Room."

"Are you kidding me?" Miriam threw her hands up in frustration.

Camille fought to hide her laughter.

With a raised eyebrow, Miriam stared at Camille. "What's funny?"

"I'm sorry Ms. Caldwell, I've just never seen you this animated, so full of life." Camille pushed her lips tight together.

"And how do you see me?" Miriam asked out of curiosity as she headed back to her seat.

Camille turned to face her. "You're just normally quiet, reserved, emotionless, but since—"

"Since what?" Miriam stared at Camille, hoping the conversation would steer anywhere else other than to where she hoped it wouldn't.

Camille paused a little longer gauging Miriam's facial expressions and body language. She knew she was teetering on the line of being too much into her boss's business, but Miriam's wide eyes suggested she wanted to know the answer. The look gave Camille the clearance to speak.

"Well, you've only been this animated since your meeting with Mr. Pierce and Mr. Lafayette. I could say that you're on edge about the promotion, but given our conversation after Mr. Lafayette questioned me about you, I think he's who has you up in arms."

"It's not him." Miriam jumped to her feet flustered yet again that her life and thoughts in recent days seemed to be centered around Shawn. "It's just this pending promotion that has me out of character, on edge. Which is why I need to get back to work. She gathered her coffee mug and laptop and moved from behind her desk. "If you'd please grab my other necessities off my desk and help me take them to the Skylight Room, that's all I'll need from you, for now."

Miriam took a deep breath before she opened the door to her office. She wasn't sure what or who was in store for her since she wouldn't be held up in her office working as she normally would. But she knew one thing for sure, she had to return to her old self, and quickly. Getting her promotion was dependent upon it.

***

Shawn had gotten the specs he needed for the time being from the blueprints stationed in the room, but knowing they had to remain there, he had the suspicion that Miriam would show up there eventually that day. For that reason alone, he decided to take residence in the room.

Calling out his name in the sexy way she did in the

staff lounge that morning had him stiff until he willed his manhood to calm down.

He wanted to ask her why she'd recited his name as she did, but with her seemingly avoiding him, he could only imagine how him pointing the moment out to her would make her retreat even more than she had been.

He smiled wide as he stared down at the papers in front of him, but again, his mind wasn't focused on his work, it was on Miriam. He heard a commotion at the door and looked up to see Miriam, wide-eyed, trying to back up out of the room, but her assistant seemed to be the barrier he needed to force her to enter the room.

"Miriam." He watched her ignore him and head straight for a chair in the corner.

He chuckled, looking at her struggle, trying to figure out how she would work in the chair with no table near it.

The only work surface available was the long, oblong mahogany conference table he sat at in the middle of the room.

He continued to look at her still struggling to stay where she was in the lone seat and no tabletop to work on.

The sunlight streaming in on her frustrated face deepened his appreciation for her beauty.

He gathered she was uncomfortable with him in the room. He was a gentleman and knew the cordial thing to do would be to let her have the room to herself for at least a little while. Give her some peace, time away from him. But he liked her too much not to be near her as often as he could.

It's not like he could get much done anyway. He had been craving the next time he would get the chance to be close to her, but then that very closeness kept him from focusing on finishing his proposal.

He wasn't trying to throw her off her game in hopes of getting the promotion, he honestly knew that with the way he'd been thinking about her, waiting to see her again, hoping to talk to her, that perhaps, this may be a good a chance as any.

She'd just have to suck it up being in the same room as him. He knew he'd enjoy soaking in her presence.

"Ms. Caldwell, would you just go over to the table? You'll never get done what you need to over here." Camille stared at Miriam clasping files in her arms and her coffee mug in her hand.

Miriam looked past Camille to see Shawn staring at her. She took a deep breath and remembered her being in the room was about her promotion. So what he was tall, handsome, and could kiss her into submission. Nope, a man had never stumped her before, and she wouldn't let one do so now.

After the number her mother did on her, she'd worked hard not to let others affect her long ago.

Shawn had temporarily knocked her off her solid ground after the earth-shattering kiss they shared but looking around the conference table with the blueprint sprawled out across it, she had to snap out of lustland and back to a focused reality to achieve her career goals.

She stood up straight and walked over to the table but chose to sit as far as she could from him. One whiff of his cologne reminded her that he was a man, a fine one at that.

Camille left the room, and Shawn found himself alone with the woman who occupied so much of his thoughts lately. He was definitely attracted to her physical aspects, but it was the traits about her he knew nothing of that plagued him so.

He cleared his throat and looked at her out the corner of his eye. He couldn't speak just yet, he was too fixated on the way she slightly bit into the pen braced on her mouth as she read. Her full lips puckered around the pen, and the way her glasses sat almost at the tip of her nose aroused him. He shook his head, trying to clear it of the improper thoughts filtering through it where Miriam was concerned.

Still reeling in his attraction to her, he loosened his tie a bit. "You know, we can at least speak to each other."

She kept her eyes focused on the papers in front of her.

"Miriam?"

"Yes, Mr. Lafayette." She refused to look up at him.

He opened his mouth to say something to her, to remind her to call him Shawn, but the conference door opened and in walked Camille.

He literally heard Miriam sigh in what seemed to be relief. It was the first time he'd seen her bear any semblance of a smile since she'd been in the room with him. Camille walked over to Miriam and leaned into her and spoke with a lowered voice.

"No, don't let her in here. I'll come out there to see her."

But whoever the *she* was didn't know Miriam didn't want her in the room. The visitor walked in. Her dark brown, slanted eyes scanned the room, and when she spotted Shawn at the table, a sneaky smile crept on her face.

Miriam rushed to the visitor and ushered her out of the room in no time.

Shawn couldn't hear much, but he did hear the name "Mimi" a few times echoing on a loud, but monotone voice. Since he'd committed Miriam's voice to his memory, he knew it wasn't Miriam calling the woman with the sneaky smile such, and Camille's voice was too mousy to have said it. It left him believing it was the dark-skinned woman calling Miriam that.

"Mimi," he mumbled to himself, smiling. The more he learned about her, the more he liked her.

"Dana, just give me my car keys and leave, please." Miriam was doing a poor job of keeping her voice low.

"Okay, okay, okay. Here. Maybe next time I'll get up even earlier so I can take the Metra to an audition."

"How'd it go?"

"I don't wanna talk about it." The woman's throaty voice sounded defeated.

Curiosity had Shawn standing at the conference room door. With it cracked and craning his neck to see into the hallway, he had a clear line of sight at the woman who soon turned her frown into a smile and shifted their conversation when she pointed towards the room. Shawn heard her final sentence. "I see why you're so flustered with him. He's fine. It'd be hard for me to focus around him too." She snickered and walked off.

He saw Miriam's chest heaving up and down. Head lowered, she took a deep breath before she walked back towards the conference room.

He practically ran back over to his seat before she made it back in. He pretended to be working when he heard the door push open, but her presence caused him to look up in hopes of making eye contact with her. As usual, she refused to look at him as she walked to her seat.

Miriam sat back down and tried to settle into her proposal, but Camille appeared at the door again. "Hey, just checking if you want your usual for lunch?"

"Yes, thanks."

"I'll be back with it in a second." She started to walk off but turned back to face Shawn. "Mr.

Lafayette?"

"Yes?" He looked up at her.

"I don't know if you made plans for your lunch already, but I know that your assistant isn't in today. Is there something you'd like me to get you, or would you rather I get your temp in here for your order?" She stood with her hands clasped in front of her and clutched her phone.

"Well, yeah, if you don't mind. I am hungry, and I can eat with Miriam." He smirked as he looked at her tight lip expression out the corner of his eye.

"I'm going to Panera Bread to pick up her lunch. Is there something there you like, or do you need a second to pull up their menu online?"

"No, I'll just have whatever Miriam is having." He loved being able to say her name so often. Given the snarl on her lips, he knew she didn't like it, but even the frown on her face was sexy to him. Any movement of her face was worth the while to him, but that deep dimple in her left cheek on display was sure to unhinge him eventually.

"You sure about that? You don't even know what she's having." Camille fought to contain her giggle. She could see from the way he smirked and looked at Miriam out the corner of his eye that he knew he was getting under her skin.

Smiling, he nodded.

"Okay. I'll be back soon enough with your orders."

Camille left the room, leaving Shawn back to his meddling thoughts of wanting to get to know more about Miriam.

It wasn't too long before he decided to engage her in a conversation. "So, is it that only those close to you are allowed to call you Mimi?"

Miriam bucked her neck, and her eyes widened as she looked up at him.

"What?" Shawn smirked. "I wasn't trying to eavesdrop earlier, but it's not like you all were quiet out there. Mimi. I like that name on you."

Miriam found herself blushing.

If she would've had the gall to answer his question, she would've told him no. Dana was the only one that called her that, and besides, her mother didn't have a nurturing bone in her body. She couldn't imagine her mother being affectionate with her. But he did say those close to her, which canceled her mother out.

Dana had called her Mimi since the first day they met, but the way it rolled off Shawn's tongue, his deep voice made her breathing pattern shift. She cursed her light almond-colored skin for making it impossible to hide her blushing.

Shawn definitely noticed it as he stared at her with a knowing look.

She cleared her throat but then looked back down at her papers. "Can we please just work in silence?

Her request didn't suit him. "So, was that like your

best friend?"

Miriam pushed her glasses up higher on the bridge of her nose as she continued typing.

She didn't know it, but he was content just staring at her. Being in the same room as her. But knowing that him asking her questions elicited facial expressions he had never seen her don before kept him firing one question after the other at her.

Abandoning working on his proposal for the moment, he sat back in his seat and stared at her. "So, were you born and raised here in Chicago?"

She kept on typing.

"Are you an only child or have loads of brothers and sisters?" He smiled.

She took a deep breath but kept busy with her proposal.

He leaned into the table and kept his eyes focused on her.

"Ever been married?"

Miriam grabbed a sticky note from the pad near her laptop, wrote FOCUS on it, and slid the note to him.

His eyes followed her hand push the blue, squared paper across the table to him, and when she removed her hand from it, he was able to fully read the lone word on it. He smiled as he picked it up and then flashed a crooked smile at her. "I am focused... on getting to know you."

The sincerity in his deep, sexy voice caused her to

look up and lock eyes with him. His admiration of her caused her to hold his gaze longer than she had planned to. Her cheeks warming up prompted her to look back down at her laptop.

She drew in a deep, slow breath as she ran her tongue across her teeth and prayed to get back lost in her work rather than dwell on how handsome he was.

Meanwhile taking in the effect he was having on her, his smile never left his face.

Camille returned with their food, saving Miriam the task of firing off at Shawn for refusing to be quiet.

Camille placed one signature brown paper bag in front of Miriam and then another in front of Shawn and placed additional napkins in between them. "Enjoy your food," she said before turning to leave.

"Wait, here, let me pay you."

"No worries." She gladly paid for his lunch without hope of compensation, knowing he was getting to her boss. She too thought Shawn would be just what Miriam needed.

"No, how much was it?"

"It's okay, it's on me." She smiled, to which Miriam looked up and eyed her suspiciously over the rim of her glasses.

"No, I insist on paying for both of our lunches." He smiled and pointed at Miriam. He handed Camille three twenties. "Keep the change."

"Enjoy your lunches." Camille gave them a wide

smile and hurried out to avoid Miriam's glaring stare.

Shawn opened his bag and began pulling the contents out. "So, I see you like grilled cheese sandwiches and tomato basil soup."

Miriam kept her eyes trained on her bag as she began taking her lunch out of it and placing the items in front of her.

He pulled the last item out of his bag. "And I see someone has a sweet tooth for their crumb cake. She did say this was your usual, so that means you eat it all the time. A lot of carbs, but you wear them well," Shawn mumbled the last of his statement. He remembered back to holding her thick, but firm, waist and although she wore loose-fitting clothes to work, she could never hide that perfectly round bottom of hers.

Miriam bit into her sandwich and chewed slowly.

Shawn took the top off his soup, gathered his spoon in his hand and was about to eat some when he remembered his ritual. He'd left his suit jacket in his office. Not worrying about possibly getting food on it, he lifted the first flap of his tie, threw it over his shoulder, and tucked the tail into his shirt.

Miriam caught his movements. The whole act looked stupid to her. *What grown man can't keep from spilling food on himself?*

Shawn looked up to see Miriam looking at him wayward. "What? All it takes is one time to have an accident right before an important meeting with no change of clothes to learn that, one, keep a spare tie and shirt with you and two, get your tie out of the way. With it like this," he tapped his tie on his shoulder, "problem solved." He commenced to eating his soup.

Miriam found herself shaking her head as she put her sandwich down and got back to typing.

"All work and no play, Miriam? At least enjoy your meal, a conversation with me before you get back to the grind."

Miriam wiped her mouth before speaking, "I would think you would want this promotion just as bad as I do, but I can't tell with all of the talking you're doing.

"Things may be given to you easily, but I have to work for what I get. So can you please leave me be? Thank you." She reached for her water bottle and gulped as much of it as she could. Being so snippy with him had left a bitter taste in her mouth.

She was normally a pleasant and docile person. Her mother's treatment toward her pushed her to be reserved, but maybe Dana and Camille were right. Shawn had caused her to be the most lively she had ever been.

With a raised eyebrow, he stared at her a little longer before he directed his attention back to his sandwich. Little did she know, nothing was given to him. He had worked hard for everything he'd gotten in life. He was still working hard for the things he wanted. She was right, he needed to focus on the task at hand.

Still not looking up, he reached for the stack of napkins in between them, but the soft, warm skin his fingers rested on let him know it wasn't paper he was touching. He slowly looked up to see Miriam looking as if she were holding her breath and her soft eyes trained on him. "Sorry, Mimi."

She held her breath, trying to suppress the tingling his touch sent through her body. She blinked rapidly before she snatched her phone off the table and scurried out of the conference room to get away from the annoyingly sexy way he called her Mimi and that tantalizing scent of his cologne.

He smirked as he got back to eating his lunch, her favorite meal.

14

With a wide grin on his face, Shawn started the engine of his car. Not because he had gotten much work done on his proposal that day, but because of his time spent with Miriam.

Even though her face often suggested she was annoyed by him, he knew with persistence, he could plow through the wall she erected between them.

Aside from her whole co-worker excuse for not dating him, he couldn't see why she wouldn't be willing to give him a chance. He was a good guy. Not bragging, he just knew he was a great catch. He was gainfully employed, grounded in who he was, ambitious, and knew he wasn't bad on the eyes.

He didn't worry too much about getting work done, it was nothing for him to burn the midnight oil. He'd do that night after night if it meant that he could spend time with Miriam. Even if she didn't talk back to him or answer any of the questions he asked her.

A few times throughout the day, he caught her in deep thought, grinding her teeth with her mouth closed. The motion made her dimple pop out. It, in conjunction with taking in the soft scent of her jasmine inspired perfume, her hazel brown eyes and the way her glasses always ended up on the tip of her nose, made her the sexiest woman he'd had the pleasure of laying his eyes on.

Trying to turn off his thoughts of Miriam, he pulled out of the company parking lot headed to happy hour at a local bar.

It was Wednesday evening and in keeping with his routine, he'd soon meet Artemis there for drinks and to catch whatever game was on one of the screens.

He settled into his seat and pressed the volume button on his steering wheel, picking back up where he left off in his 90s hip hop music playlist when his phone rang. He decided to answer it through his car speakers.

His father's voice soon filled his car. "Shawn, what are you doing?"

Vincent Lafayette didn't call him much, so he was surprised but happy to talk to his father. "Just got off work and was headed to happy hour with Artemis."

"Oh, but can you swing by the house first?"

"Is everything okay?" His father's chipper voice didn't give him room to think there was something wrong, yet he still wanted to be certain.

"Nothing's wrong. We have reason to celebrate.

We'd love to have you here for the festive occasion."

Shawn's face scrunched in bewilderment. He'd only heard that kind of happiness in his father's voice when he was doting on his brother, but he never held back on sharing good news of him, so he thought maybe the excitement his father was conveying had nothing to do with his brother. For that, he'd happily alter his plans for the evening.

"Okay, dad. I'll be there as soon as traffic lets me. Let me call Arty now and let him know I won't be meeting him."

"Okay, son. Just hurry up and get here." His father ended the call, making it easier for him to call Artemis.

Artemis picked up after five rings. He spoke loudly over the chatter of the bar. "Hey man, where are you? It's some baddies up in here. You better hurry up and get here before I claim them all."

Shawn smirked. "Whatever, man. You couldn't handle all of those women in there anyway."

"You wanna bet? Hold on Shawn, get her another one of whatever she's having…You're welcome." He lowered his voice and spoke into the phone, "Shawn, I'mma give you five more minutes to get here before all the ladies up in here are headed home with me."

"Like I said, that ain't happening. But sorry man, my dad just called and wants me to stop by the house, so I'mma head over there. I'll catch up with you another day."

"Cool. More ladies for me. Speaking of which, the one I just bought a drink for is on her way back from the bathroom now. Let me get to minding her business so I can make her my business tonight."

Shawn simply shook his head as he ended the call.

Taking a main street most of the way to cut through the city rather than bear the crowded expressway, he soon pulled up in front of his parents' two-story brick home in a southwestern suburb of Chicago. It wasn't the home where he and his brother had grown up, they grew up on the south side of Chicago, but it had been his parents' home for sixteen years. Long enough to create some notable memories there. Some good and some bad, as far as he was concerned.

He got out of his car and stretched as he looked down the tree-lined street and noticed his brother's Benz truck parked a few houses down the block from his parents' home. "This must be a pretty big surprise if Chad is already here," he said to himself as he made his way up the concrete steps.

He had a key, but he just loved ringing the doorbell knowing his mom would come answer the door and quickly engulf him in a hug. He always needed her display of affection to ground him before having to witness how much his father adored his brother.

He rang the doorbell and as expected, his mother soon pulled back a scrunched up sheer white curtain in the sliver of glass to the left side of the door to see who was there.

He had told his mom often that the door was made to be seen through so she should remove the curtains to both sides of it, but she dismissed his advice stating that although the door was pretty from the outside, everyone didn't need to know what was going on inside.

Smiling, she opened the door. "Shawn, I'm so happy to see you." She kissed his cheek and lifted on her tiptoes to wrap her arms around his neck, to which he lifted her completely off the ground.

"Put me down, boy." She laughed and swatted at him as he placed her back on her feet. "You've been lifting me off of the ground and hugging me like that since you were twelve, right after your growth spurt."

He smiled. "I can't help it that you're so short, mom."

She laughed. "Yes, you and your brother did get your height from your father and his side of the family. Come on in." She stepped aside and allowed Shawn to enter and then closed the door behind him.

"Uncle Shawn." Deja ran full speed at him with her arms up.

As always, he squatted, pretending to brace himself as if the impact of her little body colliding into his might make him topple over.

"Muah." He over-exaggerated the kissing sound as he kissed her cheek and stood up with her wrapped in his arms. "How are you, beautiful?" He pulled his head back to make eye contact with her.

She played with his tie and said, "Good." She wriggled in his arms, trying to free herself of his embrace.

He gingerly placed her down on her feet but kissed her cheek once more.

"Come on Uncle Shawn, let's go look at the cake." She could only wrap her little hand around two of his fingers as she began pulling him towards the back of the house.

"Okay," he said to his niece but with wide eyes looked back at his mother and mouthed, "Cake?"

Her eyebrows lifted as she shooed him in the direction of the kitchen.

He made it down the short hallway and into the kitchen in no time with Deja dragging him there.

"Shawn, my boy," his father said loudly as he looked up at Shawn from the granite island centered in the room. "Good, you're finally here. We can cut the cake and celebrate your brother's latest accomplishment."

Shawn's mood soured instantly as he looked up to see his father putting a makeshift crown on Chad's head.

"I'm so proud of you son." Vincent patted Chad on the back and then squeezed his shoulder as he leaned into him and kissed his forehead.

Chad turned around to look at his brother. "Bro." Chad smiled as he stood up from his stool at the island

and held one arm out.

Shawn took his time walking over to Chad and accepted his extended arm before they pulled each other in for a one-arm hug. "Chad," Shawn said, barely audible as he pulled away from his brother.

Rochelle went and stood near her son. "You know your father never passes up a chance to celebrate Chad." She chuckled as she made her way back over to a cabinet and gathered paper plates and spoons for the cake and ice cream.

"I know…all too well," he mumbled the last of his statement and it took every morsel of restraint in him not to turn around and walk right back out of the house, but Deja tugging on his finger reminded him to play nice in front of her.

"See Uncle Shawn, look at the cake grandpa got for my daddy. Isn't it cool?" Deja worked hard to climb up an empty stool situated at the island. Once there, she hunched on her knees and stared at the cake. "Can we cut it now?" Her bright, round eyes glowed as she stared at her father.

"Sure, squirt." Chad leaned over and pinched her cheek.

"That's right, let's cut into this cake, slap some ice cream on the plates and celebrate how awesome my boy is. He excels in everything he does." Vincent's smile beamed as he stepped back and folded his arms across his chest as he stared at Chad. His eyes glossed over, and he cleared the emotions from his throat before he said, "You never cease to amaze me.

"It was just last year that you started your own practice after receiving so many promotions and accolades at the hospital. Now look at you, you've won a ten-million-dollar grant for your practice because of how caring you are with patients and how knowledgeable you are in the pediatric field. I'm so glad that others see how brilliant you are as I know you to be. Those doctors were wrong, they were all wrong..." Vincent let his words trail off as he turned his back to his family and wiped his tears.

"Thank you, dad. Thank you all for always believing in me."

"Let's cut the cake," Deja demanded as her small fist hit the countertop.

Except for Shawn, they all laughed as Chad's wife put their son in his car seat and began to fix Deja's cake and ice cream.

Vincent, with a smile now on his face that reached his eyes, rejoined his wife and Chad at the island. He looked over at Shawn several feet away from everyone. "Come on over here and celebrate your brother with us."

"Hold on for a second, dad, let me take this phone call." Shawn pulled his phone out of his pocket and within seconds had it up to his ear. "Hello, hold on." He turned his back to his family and walked to the front of the house and hid in the formal living room.

He put his phone back in his pocket. No one had called him. He used the ruse to put distance between him and his dad.

Bearing witness to another one of his praise fests over Chad daunted him.

He hated how he never was able to be truly happy for his brother because he spent so much of the celebration time despising his father.

He sat down on the floral couch and dropped his head into his hands and heaved a long sigh.

He remembered back to him and his brother having basketball championship games the same day. It would be his last game ever as a high school athlete while Chad was a senior down at Duke University. Although they hoped for it, neither of the boys really knew they would make it to the finals at their schools. With them both needing to win the final games of their perspective series, they didn't know the games would fall on the same date until two days before.

With it being his last high school career game, Shawn just knew his father wouldn't let him down and would choose to be at his game. He arrived home late after practice the day before, ready to tell his father that they had already deemed him the MVP of the season and the post-season when his mom told him that his dad had hopped on the last flight of the night to Durham to make sure he wouldn't miss Chad's game that next day. Vincent had let him down again.

If that wasn't enough disappointment to rattle a teenager, two weeks later Chad announced there was an error on correspondence for his graduation ceremony. It was actually the same day as Shawn's high school graduation.

Shawn remembered sitting in the kitchen with his parents hearing Chad make the announcement on the speakerphone. His mother was disheartened, wondering how in the world she could be at both of her son's graduations when they were on the same day, thirty minutes apart in different states. Their father quickly settled the dilemma. Shawn remembered his father's words exactly. "No need to fret Ro." The nickname he'd given his wife. "You stay here and cheer on Shawn while I go and cheer on our miracle."

Shawn recalled the dumb smile on his father's face as he left the kitchen, thinking he had given the perfect solution to such a major dilemma for their family. Shawn stalked out of the kitchen with his head hung low, realizing he'd probably never get the attention from his father he desired.

Coming back to the present, Shawn sat back on the couch in the dark living room, seething that things still hadn't changed. His father never bothered to ask him how things were going for him at work, which is why he chose not to tell them he was vying for the promotion. He couldn't wait to see his father's reaction when he announced that he'd been elevated to S.E.A. He needed to see the light of admiration in Vincent's eyes for him. But hearing the joy in his father's voice as he retold a story from one of Chad's season-high games in undergrad, he knew the night would be another one solely focused on Chad.

He had to get out of there.

He got up from the couch and stretched before smoothing out his pants and adjusting his tie. He made his way back into the kitchen and walked over to Chad. "Congratulations, bro." He extended his arm and pulled Chad into a hug. "I gotta go."

Chad, looking the most like their father, looked at Shawn in confusion. "Leaving so soon?"

"Yeah, honey, you haven't even had any cake or ice cream. It really is good," his mother said, putting another forkful of the yellow cake with buttercream frosting in her mouth.

"Yeah, Uncle Shawn, it's good," Deja said without looking back as she mimicked her grandmother and forced a big spoonful of cake into her mouth.

"Okay missy, that's enough for you," Chad's wife said to Deja as she pulled her plate away from her.

"Aw, mom," Deja whined.

"Deja," Chad said with a stern voice.

"Sorry, mommy," Deja said.

"Look, guys, I really gotta go," Shawn said and turned to leave, but he felt his mother put her hand on his arm. He bent down and hugged her and kissed her forehead. The embrace almost made him stay until his father said, "Alright son…" and started on another story bragging about Chad.

He broke his embrace with his mother and rushed out of the house.

He headed home, inspired to deepen the appeal of his proposal. He couldn't help but to think that getting the promotion at work would cause his father to love him the way he loved Chad.

15

Shawn didn't sleep much the night before. He was consumed with hurt and anger after yet another one of his father's "Chad" sessions.

The only time his mood shifted to happy was when thoughts of Miriam funneled through it. He willed her to the front of his mind and then finally fell asleep, around 3 a.m., dreaming of her.

The dream was the most vivid one of them he'd experienced to date. He wished it would come true. She had called out his name so much that she was hoarse by the end of their lovemaking session. Which was a stark contrast to the silent treatment she'd kept up with him so far that day.

He made it to work, hoping to just focus on his proposal and lose sight of his issues over his father's favoritism with his brother. But remembering he'd be working on it in the conference room with Miriam excited him. He could work and play. It was a win-win for him. Since he'd come in for work so early, he thought he might have gotten a lot of the "work" out of his system before Miriam made it in, but to his delightful surprise, he walked in the room to see her typing away. He said good morning to her, but she mumbled out her response without even looking up at him.

Her not looking up at him was okay with him, it gave him a chance to thoroughly take her in before he put his belongings in the same chair he'd occupied the day before. He walked over to the floor to ceiling window facing the west, giving him a great view of the afterglow of the sunrise settling in its slow orbit. But, as magnificent as the blue hues of the skies and the tropical drops of the colors of the sun painting the sky were, it all paled in comparison to Miriam's beauty when he turned around and looked at her.

Granted, he couldn't see her face, but it was imprinted on his heart, the eyes of his mind. He'd had the celestial pleasure of kissing her, so he knew how the dip in her upper lip felt against his.

He stared at the bun securely pinned at the nape of her neck and wished he could unravel it so that he could embed his fingers deep into her hair as he stared into her hazel eyes. She was meant to be adored.

He smirked at how her loose-fitting blouse hung off her shoulders. *Why is she trying to hide that banging body of hers? Does she not want her perky breasts up for discussion during the workday? Okay, maybe not.* And he knew they were since he'd mistakenly touched them in search of her face before they kissed.

He looked down at how the hem of her pants easily went past her flats. He laughed out loud, causing her to shift in her seat and rub her neck as if she was tense.

He stepped forward but stopped himself from moving any further. He was ready and willing to massage the knots out her neck if need be, help her loosen up and not just with his hands. He'd enlist his tongue to do the job as well.

He remembered her storming out of the room the day before after his barrage of questions. Her sudden exit gave him a great view of her meaty butt as she left. The woman was in for a rude awakening if she thought her baggy clothes actually hid her curves and kept her banging body under the radar of men ogling her around the office.

Baggy pants or not, he knew she had ample thighs with the way they spread across her seat as he continued staring at her. He could've watched her forever, but her voice brought him back to the moment.

"Not that I care, and I shouldn't since you're my competition, but are you going get to work or not?" She never lifted her head from her laptop.

He smiled. She had to have cared to make such a statement. He walked over to his seat at the table, ready to get to know her more while they worked. Maybe her little speech was her subliminal way of getting him to talk to her. He would capitalize on the moment.

He sat down, opened his laptop, and asked her question after question, for hours, to which she didn't open her mouth until Camille came in the room.

"Ms. Caldwell, you ready for me to order your lunch?"

"Yes, I'm starving," she said in an exasperated voice.

His groin tightened. He was starving to taste her again. He wished he could feast on her right then and there on the big conference room table.

"I didn't eat breakfast and had an early dinner before burying myself in this proposal the rest of the night."

I knew she was a workaholic. Shawn looked at her out the corner of his eye. He loved to hear the sweet melody of her voice. He hoped Camille could keep her talking since he was unsuccessful in getting a peep out of her since the one question she'd asked that morning.

"So, what will it be, the usual?" Camille said.

"Do you ever try anything new?" Shawn asked, sincerely.

Miriam snapped her neck at him, ready to tear into him for his snooping into her business, but quickly realized the behavior would be out of her character. She redirected her attention to Camille, whose eyes were still bulging as if she too were shocked by Shawn's question. She opened her mouth to speak, but Shawn's voice elevated above hers.

"I forgot, you do. Something for which I'm extremely grateful for." His smile grew wide as he looked down at his laptop, deciding to ignore the deathly stare she shot his way.

Miriam's nostrils flared as she stared at him. Why did he get under her skin so? He was grateful for their kiss? She wasn't.

It had kept her restless most nights since it happened. The intense passion between them during the kiss was like a television show marathon playing in her mind ever since. Only the writers had taken the passion between the two of them from the studio to her bedroom. The things he did to her body in her dreams made her squeeze her legs tighter as she took deep breaths to even her breathing. When she felt her heart rate was back at a normal pace, she looked at Camille and said, "Yes, I'll take my usual. I know what I'm getting with it." She turned her attention back to her laptop.

Camille stood with her lips pressed tight trying to hide her amusement of the duo.

"Camille, if you don't mind getting it for me, I'd like what Miriam is having too. It's good."

Miriam stiffened at the lilt in his voice at the end of his statement. It suggested more than his words had spoken. Her nipples hardened, and the need to squeeze her legs even tighter emerged. She shut her eyes for a moment, trying to clear her thoughts.

She opened them to see him smirking, staring at her, to which she quickly turned her head and looked at Camille.

"Well, I'll be back with your orders soon enough," Camille said, a few puffs short of full-on laughter.

"I'm not that bad, you know?" Shawn said as he looked up at Miriam who still refused to look in his direction. He decided to give up for the moment and try to focus on his proposal, although he was finding the necessary task hard since Miriam's subtle scent kept permeating his senses.

But he had to reel his thoughts back in. Forcing himself to focus on his screen, he didn't look up at her again.

Shawn had been speechless for about ten minutes before Miriam realized the odd silence surrounding her.

She'd never admit it to him, or barely herself for that matter, but the smooth tenor in his voice had become like a soundtrack for her to work to. Although she'd never answer any of the too personal questions he'd been asking her. He didn't need to know any of the stuff he asked her about herself. It's not like they'd ever be a couple.

Or would they?

Looking at him for a few seconds and noting the

quizzical look on his face that seemed to submerge him in his work, she allowed herself to study his features. The softer side of her wished she could reach out and caress that strong jawline of his or run her fingers over the ripples of waves in his close-cropped haircut. A smile slowly inched across her face relishing in the memories of their kiss. Instinctively, her fingers patted her lips as if they'd just kissed.

"Miriam. Mimi."

"Ms. Caldwell?"

Miriam was brought out of her sensual reverie by the sounds of Shawn and Camille's voices, respectively, and their stares.

She'd lost it again. Thoughts of pleasure at his lips had unraveled her again in front of him. She stiffened in her chair, unsure of whether or not she'd called out his name in delight as she had the day before.

Camille treaded lightly towards Miriam and placed her bag of food in front of her. She'd already given Shawn his. The unspoken chemistry between the two, on Miriam's part, had been giving Camille much-needed excitement over the past couple of days. "Here you are." Camille patted the bag in front of Miriam and sealed her lips to keep any sound effects of amusement at bay.

Miriam pulled Camille down to her and leaned into her as she whispered, "What just happened? Did I say something?" She cleared her throat but kept her voice low. "Did I say his name?"

Camille chuckled at her boss. "No, you didn't say anything. You were just staring at him."

Miriam cupped her mouth, not wanting Shawn privy to any part of their conversation. "Did he see me staring at him."

"Yes, I think he did."

Miriam dropped her head in her hands.

Camille wanted to probe her boss more about the matter, but she thought against it. Although Miriam had been informal with her here and there, she wasn't certain how, and if, Miriam would take a liking to her bringing up Shawn. Especially since she was hell-bent on declaring she didn't like him. She settled on saying, "Is that all?"

"Yes, or you could just shoot me now," Miriam mumbled.

"What?" Camille's eyebrows lifted.

"Never mind. That'll be all," Miriam said.

"Okay. Just text me if you need anything else." Camille nodded at Shawn and left the room quietly.

Shawn emptied the contents of his bag, but again, before he dug in, he flipped the top flap of his tie over his shoulder and bit the corner of his bottom lip as he tucked the tail into his shirt.

She snuck a peek at him during the ritual. The day before, she found the act childish, but still experiencing the aftermath of her brief but vivid daydream, she found his way of keeping his tie clean, sexy. She didn't know where the sudden thought of him tying her hands with it in a bedroom scene came from. *What is he doing to me?*

She didn't get a chance to toil any further with her thoughts because Shawn's voice beckoned her attention.

"Mimi, I can see why this is your favorite meal. It's really good. It was good yesterday, and it's still good today."

Embarrassed by why she'd been staring at him, she couldn't bring herself to look up at him or respond to him.

He ignored the fact that she hadn't responded back to him and decided to continue with his inquisition. "So, is this the only thing you've ever wanted to do?" He spread his hands across the blueprints laid out in front of them.

If it were anyone else that had asked her that question, she would've talked their ear off nonstop in response to how she breathed architecture, engineering, and design, but she couldn't be that open with Shawn.

"Okay, do you like sports?"

No answer from her.

"Ever broke a bone?"

Silence.

"Are you an early bird or a night owl?"

Only the tapping of fingers against her keyboard could be heard.

"Favorite place to vacation?"

Miriam picked up her sandwich, took another bite of it, rubbed her hands together to free it of crumbs and then went back to typing on her laptop.

"Favorite TV show? Dream car? Or do you already own it? What website do you visit the most? What's your biggest fear? Biggest accomplishment?"

He looked at her as her chest deflated from exhaling a deep breath.

"You know I can keep this up all day." He smirked.

If it weren't for his deep voice sending chills up her spine frequently, she could ignore him all day, but she needed him to stop talking already. She needed to focus. She thought he needed to as well.

"Mimi, why won't you answer any of my questions? Afraid you might enjoy actually holding a conversation with me?"

She heard a faint vibrating noise and saw him pull his phone from his pocket.

Focusing on his phone allowed her to focus on properly breathing again. His question had startled her. *Does he know that my body is having reactions to him against my will? But he hasn't said anything about my slip-ups yet. Lord, please don't let him bring them up.*

She stared at him as she watched a scowl mar his handsome face. He stuffed his phone back in his pocket, got up from his seat, threw away his food, although he'd only gotten through half of it, and returned to his seat without even a glance in her direction.

He stayed that way with her throughout the rest of the workday.

It was early evening and the natural light outside paled in comparison to the lighting in the conference room. Miriam powered down her computer and frowned at the knowledge that she'd gotten what she wanted from him while they worked, silence. But it had been eerie compared to his barrage of questions moments before he checked his phone.

He'd asked me questions that suggested he really wanted to get to know me and I refused to answer them, so why was his silence so daunting?

He had been too quiet the rest of the day. At times, she found herself ready to ask him if he was okay, but the stern look on his face, his eyebrows practically touching each other the rest of the day, led her to believe it was best to say nothing to him.

But who was she kidding? She hadn't been able to focus since he had stopped talking to her during lunch.

***

Shawn was perfectly content with the pace he moved at on his proposal the earlier part of the day. Granted, he hadn't done much on the proposal since he was trying his best to get Miriam to open up to him, especially during lunch, but one Facebook notification had changed that for him. It was an alert that his dad had posted pics of Chad's celebration the night before. One in particular plagued him.

In it, his father had a wide grin as he stood next to Chad. The caption read how proud he was of his son's latest accomplishment.

Social media wasn't the rave the last time Shawn had done something his father should have considered noteworthy, like graduating with dual degrees in architectural design and architectural engineering, but he still had no memorabilia of his dad gloating over him and his accomplishments.

The picture brought back to the forefront of his mind that he needed to focus. Seeing the picture, the public display of adoration for his brother from his dad, was just what he needed to end his "getting to know you" fest with Miriam and focus on crafting a surefire proposal that his boss and the hotel owner would have no choice but to pick.

He rubbed his eyes after having stared between the screen and the blueprints nonstop. Looking over to the window, he could see the sun was setting outside and he caught a glimpse of Miriam. Still beautiful, she was busy neatly wrapping the cord on her laptop charger.

Should I say something to her? Explain why I got quiet on her earlier? Pick up where I left off with my questions from earlier? Offer to walk her to her car? He decided to do so, but the frosted door to the conference room opened and thwarted his attempt.

"Good, you're both still here," Mr. Pierce said walking in, just as chipper as he was the day he announced they both were up for the promotion.

"Yeah, we were just heading out. I know I was. What about you, Miriam?" Shawn looked over at her and held her stare. She looked shocked that he'd spoken to her again and that annoyed him. He didn't want her thinking he stopped talking to her earlier because he lost interest in her. Maybe he would walk her to her car so he could explain himself to her.

She looked away with questions lingering in her eyes. "Yes, I'll be leaving as soon as I pack up here and get my things from my office," she said to Mr. Pierce.

"Just hold on a second, you two. I was on my way out when I got a call from Mr. Schaeffer. Remember, he's the owner of the hotels either of you will be redesigning?"

"Of course," Shawn said.

"Of course, I remember who he is," Miriam said with a hint of merriment in her voice.

"Well, he's requesting that the two of you join him at his home on the Isle of Palms Beach in Charleston for the weekend."

Miriam's eyes widened. She rubbed the back of her neck.

Shawn smiled, thinking about the possibility of

being on the beach with Miriam. *Will she let her hair down? Will I get to see her in a bikini?* The thought of seeing her in just a few strings to support small patches of material covering her private areas made his manhood enlarge.

Mr. Pierce chuckled. "I see you're excited about this news, Shawn, but Miriam, your deer-caught-in-headlights expression suggests otherwise."

"Oh no, Mr. Pierce, I'm excited about the chance to meet Mr. Schaeffer. I guess I just don't wear my happiness like others."

"It's alright, my dear. He says he wants you two to see how he lives and to incorporate personal touches of his life into the design of the chain."

"I can understand, but he sent us specifics about him. And I know I did enough research on him to infuse his personal style into the hotels," Miriam asserted.

"He knew at least one of you would say that, but he insists that you *see* how he lives."

"Okay," Miriam said.

"So, you'll arrive there tomorrow evening. He has an agenda prepared for you all for the weekend. You'll present your proposals Sunday, and he will choose which one he wants to go with."

Miriam cleared her throat. "I'm sorry Mr. Pierce, did you say we'll be presenting our proposals to him Sunday?"

"Yes."

"But I thought they weren't due for another week?" Miriam asked.

"Yes, that was the case, but he's ready to make some moves now. We have to be ready to flow with him, or else he may seek out another firm. And besides, with your track record, I'm certain you're more than prepared to present to him on Sunday."

Miriam pressed her lips tight together, working to keep a straight face. A cool demeanor.

"Well, my assistant will email you all your travel details tonight. Again, good luck to the both of you." Mr. Pierce left the room as quickly as he had entered it.

Shawn fixed his gaze on Miriam. "So, I guess we'll be seeing one another a lot this weekend." He didn't try to hide the wry smile on his lips.

Miriam gave him a nervous half-smile before grabbing her belongings and rushing out of the conference room.

16

Miriam rushed through her front door and slammed it shut. She leaned back with her back flat against it as if someone had chased her up the six flights of stairs to her condo. Chest still heaving, she kept a tight grip on the strap of her messenger bag on her shoulder.

Dana eyed her suspiciously from the couch facing the door. "Are you okay? Was someone chasing you?" Dana stood to her feet and rested her hands on her hips.

"No, nothing like that." Rattled, Miriam took a deep breath before pushing herself off the door with the sole of her foot. Thoughts of possibly being in such close proximity to Shawn all weekend worried her. Not to mention her proposal was due a week early.

She was heading straight to her room when Dana jumped out in front of her. "Where are you going?"

"To my room."

"But you're coming back out, right? Have dinner

that I made, right?"

"No. I have to pack, and then I'm gonna call it a night."

Miriam tried to walk around Dana, but Dana spread her arms out wide, blocking Miriam from getting past her.

"Pack? Where are you going?"

"To Charleston. The Isle of Palms Beach," Miriam said absentmindedly and finally pushed past Dana. She walked into her room hoping to close the door behind her, but with Dana so close on her heels, the act remained a thought.

"What are you going to Charleston for and when are you leaving?" Dana asked as her voice elevated to a level of excitement Miriam hoped would leave it soon.

"For work and I leave tomorrow," Miriam mumbled as she took her flats off and walked into her closet.

"It's a work trip, which means you get to discuss all things architecture. You haven't gone away for work in a while. Normally you're so excited about them. Why the sour face now, girlie?"

"I don't want to talk about it," Miriam mumbled as she appeared from her closet with oversized slacks and blouses. She dropped the outfits on her bed, then went back in her closet to retrieve her mid-sized suitcase.

Dana's eyes bulged. "You don't wanna talk about architecture?" She got up from Miriam's firm bed, walked over to her friend, and put the back of her hand up to her forehead. "You sick? Running a fever? Because you not wanting to talk about architecture must mean that you're delirious at the moment."

Miriam pulled her head out of Dana's reach. "No, I'm not delirious. I just don't want to talk about it." She let out a loud sigh and went to her dresser to get her undergarments, her signature bloomers and full cotton bras.

Dana stared at Miriam sulking, and then her eyes brightened as if she had an epiphany. "Wait a minute. You're going on a work trip, and you're not ecstatic about it?" She pointed an accusing finger at Miriam. "Could it be that a certain great kisser will be going on this trip and you're unsure if you'll be able to keep your lips off of him?" Dana laughed as Miriam tightened her mouth and stared at her with her hands on her hips. "What?" Dana's laughter finally subsided. "Tell me that I'm lying."

"You are." Miriam found herself rolling her eyes at Dana before she flopped down on her bed, pushing the pile of clothes she just laid on it out of her way. "Yes, he'll be there, but I'm not worried about Shawn." Her voice shook with annoyance. My boss just told me today that the proposal is due this Sunday and not next Friday like he originally told us."

Dana went and stood in front of her. "Miriam, I know you and how hard you've been working on this proposal. You do this kind of stuff in your sleep, so I know the proposal isn't what's bothering you. And while I know why you want the promotion, that isn't it either."

"Oh, really? So, tell me what my problem is Ms. Know-It-All."

"I'll tell you what your problem is, Mimi." Dana cocked her neck with a defiant look on her face. "You've gone under the radar all these years with men. Hiding that stunning figure of yours under those baggy clothes you wear, but now a man has seen you. Seems like he sees the real you and you can't take it."

"The real me?" Miriam's face scrunched in confusion. "You don't know what you're talking about. He doesn't know me to have seen the real me."

"You silly rabbit, don't you know the power that kisses hold?" Dana said wide-eyed.

"They do not," Miriam spat. The subject matter was new territory for her, and she certainly didn't want Shawn to have any power over her. Or was it too late for that?

"Be honest with yourself, before knowing who you were kissing, with how you were kissed, did you feel a connection with him? I mean deeper than lust."

Miriam refused to answer the question.

"Was the kiss rushed or did he take his time like he was on a quest to understand you? What made you tick? Did your skin tingle from his touch? Did you feel safe in his arms? Did you feel like he knew your story and you wanted to know every aspect of his life?"

Miriam had a far off look in her eyes as she ran her fingers across her lips.

"Clearly, you won't answer those questions out loud. But it seems like you do have the answers." Dana continued on believing she was right. "And even after knowing who he was, does your body still react to him whenever he's near? Does his voice do something to you? His smell? His smile? Do you want to get to know more about him? Does he come to your mind at the oddest times of the day?"

"No. I couldn't possibly be into him from just a kiss." Miriam wanted Dana to stop bombarding her with the silent ailments she had been experiencing since kissing Shawn. She wanted to keep the symptoms of their kiss foreign to everyone, especially to herself.

"Au contraire, mon amie. Being thoroughly kissed by the right guy shifts your breathing pattern. It can shift your outlook on life. It can scare you because you didn't know it was what, and by who, you needed. It excites quieted places in you. Let go of fear and embrace the possibilities Shawn can offer you."

Miriam jumped to her feet ready to squash the feelings and thoughts Dana's meddling tirade had incited in her. "The only thing Shawn can offer me is a congratulations after I get this promotion." She grabbed a blouse off the bed to fold.

Dana snatched it from her.

"What are you doing?" Miriam asked.

"Helping you," Dana said.

"How? You're gonna fold my clothes and pack them for me?"

"No, I'm helping you by not letting you take these obtuse pieces of fabric on a trip that involves a beach."

"Give me my shirt." Miriam reached out to grab the lavender button-up blouse that was honestly two sizes too big for her.

"No." Dana swerved around Miriam, quickly grabbed the other clothes from the bed and threw them out the bedroom door into the hallway.

Miriam's eyes widened with shock. "Why did you do that?"

"Because I had to."

"But I need my work clothes for this trip."

"Haa. You shouldn't be wearing those to work, and you definitely won't be wearing them any day of this trip. Beaches call for sundresses and bikinis."

"But I have meetings I need to dress for."

"Having invited you to his beach house, I'll just go out on a limb and say that he wants everything to be more casual this weekend."

"You don't know that for certain."

"You're right, I don't. But let's have you pack for the casual scenario."

Miriam gave up on trying to get past Dana to get

her things from the hallway. Shoulders slumped, she walked back over to her bed and flopped down on it. "So what should I take then? I have the same style and size clothes in different colors."

Dana shook her head. "Glad you're finally seeing things my way. We'll do something about your wardrobe when you get back, but for now, we'll improvise." Dana walked into Miriam's closet and rummaged through it until she found what she was looking for. "Aha! I knew my shopping spurts for you over the years would pay off." Dana brought a bag of clothes out of the closet with her.

Miriam covered her face.

"What?" Dana asked, confused.

"I knew I should've just given away those tight-fitting clothes you've sent me over the years when you lived in New York and then trekked across the country to California to pursue your dancing career."

Dana frowned at the mention of her dance dreams, but not wanting to further the conversation, she allowed a smirk to wash over her face. She laid her hand flat over her chest and feigned being appalled. "Why would you have done such a thing? Everything I sent you over the years were heartfelt gifts. I had you in mind with each outfit."

"No, you had the mind to try and change the way I dress."

"No, I just wanted you to live a little. Lose the

oversized clothes, put on something form-fitting, go out and enjoy yourself instead of being cooped up in the house weekend after weekend watching architecture documentaries."

Miriam sighed, wanting to end the conversation.

"Let's see." Dana flipped the bag over, emptying it. "Oh, I remember getting this one in L.A. She held up a coral-colored spaghetti strap sundress."

"I tried that one on when you sent it, it's too tight around my butt." Miriam frowned.

"Perfect." Dana winked. "Your waist is trim, and when you say tight, I know you mean it actually fits you."

Dana folded a few more sundresses, Bermuda shorts and dainty tank tops, and put them in the open luggage near the bed. "Okay, so the only thing left to do is to pack shoes, underwear, and a bikini."

"You threw my underwear in the hallway."

"Darling, you have no business taking those granny panties and junior high sports bras with you on a weekend getaway. They can stay right in the hallway, better yet, burn to ashes." Dana went over to Miriam's top drawer on her dresser and grabbed the delicate garments in the back of it. "I also knew me dragging you to Victoria's Secret for their annual sale would pay off." She gave a wry smile as she stretched out a pair of black lace thongs and waved them in the air.

"I am not wearing those or any of the other ones

you have in your hand," Miriam said.

"Yes, you will. I better not find out you were traipsing on the beach with a sexy, fitted sundress and bloomers underneath." Dana went and dropped the bra and panty sets into the luggage.

"Now to find those bikinis I made you buy at the store closeout last summer when I was here." Dana headed back to the closet when Miriam's sudden movements stopped her.

Miriam jumped up from the bed. "I am not wearing a bikini. I don't care how much water and sand there'll be in sight. I will not be around Mr. Schaeffer and Shawn half-naked. With as many questions as he's asked me these past days, I don't wanna give him any other topics he'll feel he'll need to discuss with me."

Dana turned to face Miriam with the widest smile her face could churn out. "Like what, that tattoo of an eagle on your left shoulder I dared you to get in undergrad. And did you just hear how you said his name? It rolled off your tongue like you treasured saying it. Like a schoolgirl trying to deny to her friends a certain boy is her crush. You do like him. You just won't admit it. And being around him this weekend is what has you flustered."

Miriam walked to her door and opened it. "Would you just get out already?"

Dana laughed. "Nope. Not until I pack your bikinis." Dana rummaged through the closet for them, but her search came up empty. She came back out with her hands on her hips and pouting. "Now where did you put them? You really aren't the type to throw things away." Dana stared at Miriam, demanding she tell her where the bikinis were.

Exhausted from Dana's antics, she huffed and pointed to the chest at the foot of her bed.

Dana smiled as she walked to it and lifted the top. She grabbed the first three bikinis she saw and rushed to put them in the luggage before Miriam fought her on the matter. She looked at her once she stood up from bending over the luggage.

"I just hope you do right and actually wear what I packed for you. And to play nice with you, I'll even pack a business casual outfit for you." Dana went in the closet and returned with items still bearing tags. She folded the sole pair of slacks and button-up blouse that actually framed Miriam's curves. She also placed three pairs of flat sandals, a pair of wedges, a pair of gym shoes, and espadrilles in her luggage.

"I'm only going away on this business trip for three days, but thanks mom for packing a week's worth of clothes for me."

"If I didn't hear the sarcasm dripping from your voice, I'd think you were sincere. But you're welcome anyway," Dana said.

Miriam eagerly switched gears. "We've spent all of this time talking about me, but how did your audition go today?"

"I don't wanna talk about it." Dana headed for the bedroom door.

"So, you can be all up in my business, but I can't be in yours?" Miriam asked.

"Good night." There was an agitation in Dana's voice as she left the room and closed the door hard behind her.

Miriam shook her head as she looked over at her luggage full of clothes she had no intentions of packing when she'd made it home.

She stripped her clothes off and threw them in her laundry hamper before making her way into her bathroom. She turned on the shower and instantly, the hot water made the bathroom foggy.

She stepped in it and let the water beat on her back as she thought about her day. Dana's evening antics had been a distraction for what plagued her while she was at work.

Yes, finding out her proposal was due that weekend was a shocker. Knowing she'd be away with Shawn for the weekend was nerve-racking, but what really stumped her was Shawn's lack of interest in her the latter part of the day. How quiet he had been after he had put his phone back down during lunch. What made the matter worse was that she even cared that he hadn't talked to her.

17

Shawn walked into the office that morning grateful that Miriam didn't answer his questions the day before or even present the opportunity for him to walk her to her car. He knew any more intimate time spent with her would draw him even closer to her. His attraction to her was growing stronger, but with the proposal deadline having been moved up, he had no choice but to buckle down and solidify his proposal that day.

He didn't know what Mr. Schaeffer had in store for them that weekend and didn't want to chance trying to prep his proposal there. He'd get done what he could at work and simply add in details he may come up with interacting with Mr. Schaeffer over the weekend.

He walked into the conference room that morning to see Miriam already sitting at the table. Although her beauty beckoned him to spark up a conversation with her, lock eyes with her if nothing but for a brief moment, he ignored the tug to do so and headed to his usual seat at the table.

Though a great deal of resilience on his part, they worked in silence until it was time to leave the building and head to the airport.

He stood up, stretched, and stared at his watch. "You ready to head out?" He looked at her, still typing away. His question went unanswered. "Miriam?"

She didn't look up but finally decided to respond, "I'll get there in time for the flight."

"I know you declined Mr. Pierce's offer to haul you to the airport on the company's dime, so did I, but I was thinking, maybe we could share a cab or an Uber to the airport? Or I could drive?

"You leave your car here, I drop you off at departures, park my car in a lot, and meet you at the gate. I'd definitely bring you back here to your car Monday morning once we get back." His naturally kempt yet thick eyebrows lifted as he stared at her.

She remained speechless as she typed.

He couldn't help himself, he chuckled at how cute she was ignoring him. "So, I take that as a no?"

She pecked a key hard one last time before powering down her laptop. She finally worked up the nerve to look up at him.

The intensity in his eyes always twisted her insides in an unnerving way. The kind of reaction that let her know her body enjoyed his presence even though her head thought otherwise. She took a deep breath, trying to even her breathing.

She couldn't afford a shaky voice when talking to him. She didn't need there to be any sign that he affected her. "No thanks, I'll get myself there and in time." She stood up, pulled up her overly loose-fitting pants and began to pack her laptop and files.

He smirked as she kept her head low as she gathered her belongings. He grabbed his and gave his limbs a final stretch after having sat for so long. "Well, I guess I'll see you on the plane."

Her body stiffened, realizing they would be on the same plane together heading to Charleston.

She closed her eyes and said a brief, silent prayer that she wouldn't be seated next to him. With his track record, she was certain that he'd try to engage her in conversation, probably the whole way there if they were next to each other. And Lord knows she couldn't take being so close to him in those tight plane seats. With his knees touching hers, shoulder to shoulder with him, and the constant whiffs of his enticing cologne might cause her to unravel in front of him, lean over and kiss him again. "Bye," she said to his back as he took slow steps out of the conference room.

Shawn dropped his laptop on the desk in his office when he made it in there. He shook his head, reflecting on how Miriam seemed hell-bent on ignoring any advances for him to get to know her more.

For heaven's sake, she wouldn't accept a free ride to the airport with him knowing that the traffic in Chicago heading to Midway airport on a Friday night would be chaotic.

His bags were packed, and he was ready to head to the airport, but his phone vibrating in the holster on his hip thwarted his attempt to grab his garment and duffle bags from behind the door.

He looked down at his phone, unsure of who the caller from New York was but decided to answer anyway. "Hello," he said with a hint of curiosity in his voice.

"Yes, may I speak with Shawn Lafayette?"

"This is he."

"Good. This is Mark Donner, producer of 'The Kissing Game'."

Unsure of why he was receiving a call from Mark, he paused before speaking. "…Okay."

"I hope I'm not interrupting your Friday afternoon, but I really needed to talk to you as soon as possible."

"Okay, I have a minute to spare." Shawn folded his arms across his chest as he prepared himself to listen to Mark.

"I'll get straight to it. You were there, you were the one kissing her, so you know how hot the kiss was, but man I have to tell you, it looks even better on camera. After scrolling through hours upon hours of footage of kisses, the kiss you shared with Miriam Caldwell was the most passionate and vibrant one we have on film.

"To be honest with you, we know that it will garner the highest viewing audience and we want to market it as such. We don't just want to leave it at airing the kiss. We want to be able to show viewers how the kiss led to you two falling in love. You two are together now, aren't you?"

"I wish." Shawn sighed and rubbed his forehead.

"Hunh?" Mark asked, unsure of what Shawn had said.

"Nothing, but what are you asking?"

"If you two are together?"

"Not that part, about the *us* falling in love part."

"Oh, we want to film you two lovebirds again. We want to interview you all on how your love has blossomed after the kiss."

"Mark, I hate to disappoint you, but Miriam and I aren't together. We're not a couple." *Not yet, at least.* Shawn didn't even bother sharing his hopes with Mark.

Dumbfounded, Mark sat back in his office chair. "I don't get it. I just knew after a kiss like that, you two would *know* that you were for each other. Especially with you all knowing each other before the kiss. Why hasn't either of your light bulbs turned on yet? Oh, this is even more reason to air you all after the kiss. Maybe we could make it live and have America phone in and tweet to help you all see you should be together."

Maybe so. Shawn stepped back to his desk and

rested on it, stretching his legs out in front of him and continued listening to Mark.

"I'm telling you, it was one thing to witness it live, but with each playback and edit, we saw just how in sync you two were with one another. We know it's love whether either of you will admit it or not. That kiss was simply magical. We want to be able to tell, share with the viewers more details of you all after they see the explosive kiss. But we need more camera time, a post-interview with you all to do that."

The more Shawn thought about it, the more he liked the idea of the interview. "I'm game to do it, but I'm not sure Miriam will be up for it. Have you contacted her yet?"

"With all of the footage we've had to sort through, we just finished editing you all last night. Contacting you all was our number one priority today. We have been trying to reach her all day with no luck."

"It'll be a stretch, maybe even impossible, but since we'll be out of town together for work this weekend, I may have enough encounters with her to convince her to do the interview. I'd love to corner her and force her to talk about the kiss."

"Out of town? Exactly where will you all be?" Mark asked.

"In Charleston, South Carolina on the Isle of Palms Beach."

Mark jumped out of his seat in delight. "You won't

believe it, but we're filming there this weekend. It would be the perfect situation, taping-wise, if we could interview you all there."

"I'll see if I can convince her to do the show, but I have to admit the likelihood of that happening is well into the negatives of never. Especially since she refuses to talk to me about the kiss, about exploring an *us*, shoot, she barely says hello to me." Shawn shook his head in frustration that he hadn't spent time wooing her since they kissed.

"Okay, well, you keep pressing her and we'll keep reaching out to her and maybe she'll fold before the weekend is over. And if you convince her before we do, please call me back at this number ASAP. This is my direct line."

"Okay, hopefully, I'll have good news for you soon." He looked down at his watch. It was 1:00 p.m. and his flight was scheduled to take off at 4:15 p.m. "I gotta go Mark. I need to get to the airport for my flight."

"Okay, bye."

Shawn ended the call feeling hopeful that things would work out in his favor that weekend.

18

Thankfully, Shawn made it to the airport and to his gate just in time for his boarding group's entry onto the plane. He was three people behind Miriam as he worked to catch his breath from the sprint he made to the gate. He was in shape alright, but trekking across Midway's expansive real estate with his bags in tow still proved challenging, even for his conditioned lungs.

He smiled as he was able to steal a glance at her phone screen she had enlarged to scan the QR code once she walked up to the gate agent. It revealed that she would be seated next to him. He looked forward to the plane ride giving him enough time to get to know her more and perhaps even convince her to go on the show again for the post-interview.

Soon he was in the long line of passengers in the jet bridge waiting to board the aircraft. Sitting in business class meant he didn't have to go that far back on the plane. Six rows from the door and he was at his seat. When he made it to his seat, the wide-eyed stare Miriam gave him let him know she wasn't all too happy about their seating arrangements.

She sat next to the window, and he watched her shrink closer and closer to it as he put his carry-on bags in the overhead compartment.

He planned to make the best of the opportunity, though.

He sat down and took a deep breath before he turned a sexy smile to her. "I didn't know we'd be sitting next to each other, but I'm glad we are."

That was it. Sitting that close to him, inhaling his cologne, and hearing his deep voice made her body tingle the same way it had when they kissed. The plane hadn't even taken off and she felt some kind of way, so she knew her senses couldn't handle being close to him for over another hour. Her body hadn't recovered from his touch from over a week before, so a slight rubbing of their knees or feeling the heat of his breath on her neck, if he dared to lean over and whisper to her, might cause her to combust right in her seat.

His presence always gave her body an experience.

Nope. She knew she couldn't sit next to him on the flight.

She lifted out of her seat and strained her neck looking around the plane for any other available seat, but the long line of people still in the aisle soon filled up the remaining empty seats on the plane.

Shawn knew why she searched the plane as she did. It didn't annoy him though. He could easily tell she was worth the chase and was willing to go to any lengths to convince her they could work as a couple.

Their first kiss proved to him that they belonged together. Not a fan of kissing, he'd done his fair share of it over the years as an act of foreplay, but never before had he not only felt the explosions in his body the way he did while kissing Miriam, but he'd never questioned his future with the woman he was kissing.

Kissing Miriam made him wonder how she'd look walking down the aisle towards him, how their kids would turn out, or any other future related questions with her. Miriam made him see his life past the promotion.

Maybe laughing at her wouldn't help to win her over, but he just couldn't contain the chuckles constantly erupting from him considering her behavior thus far on the plane.

Seeing there were no other seats available on the plane, she shoved her headphones in her ears, angled her body away from his, and closed her eyes as she made the wall her companion until well after they landed.

During deplaning, he insisted on helping her with her luggage, but when he accidentally touched her while trying to assist with her bags, he knew from the stunned look in her eyes that his touch elicited a cataclysmic response from her body. It had done the same to him.

His eyes trailed from her face to her heaving chest, then back up to her cautious eyes. He could tell she was trying to settle her breathing as his hand remained on top of hers, gripping her bag.

She opened her mouth to speak, but words never passed her full, brown lips before she snatched her bag and rushed to deplane.

He didn't rush after her as they headed to the spot they would be picked up from at arrivals.

There was a weighted silence between them as they rode to Mr. Schaeffer's three-story beach house. Miriam didn't hesitate to jump out of the car, and seemingly away from him, barely before the driver even put the Town Car in park.

Shawn kept an arm's length distance from her as they walked the pebbled path up to the steps and to the front door of the house. By the time they made it there, a petite, Hispanic woman opened the door. "Hello, come in."

Soon Mr. Schaeffer entered the foyer with his wife not too far behind him. "Hello, Miriam." He extended his hand out and shook hers. "Hello, Shawn." He gave Shawn a firm handshake. "So glad you all took me up on the offer to join me this weekend."

Shawn nodded his head. Mr. Pierce's announcement for the weekend didn't sound like an offer that could be passed over. It seemed more like a requirement. Shawn peeked over at Miriam who had put a sizable distance between them. She looked poised to speak, but Mr. Schaeffer carried on.

"I didn't just invite you all here to get a peek at how I live, learn more about my tastes, I wanted to become more acquainted with the person who'd be responsible for designing what I expect to be my next empire. If your looks are any indication of your design minds, then choosing a design may be a tough decision for me after all. I mean what, with your strapping looks..." He looked to Shawn then over to Miriam. "...and your pure beauty, I expect this to be a tough decision."

"Oh, Barry, leave them alone. Can't you see you're making her blush?" his wife said.

Miriam was blushing alright, but not from Mr. Schaeffer's compliment, but from the heated stare Shawn had fixed on her. She foolishly looked over at Shawn when Mr. Schaeffer complimented his looks. He held her stare at first with a look of admiration in it, but he soon turned the dial up on his oven of interest in her. Charleston's high temps and summer humidity was no match for the way his approval of her made her skin sear.

Mr. Schaeffer's wife walked forward and touched Miriam's arm, pulling her gaze away from Shawn. "Don't mind my husband. I'm Julie Ann, and it's a pleasure to meet you." She squeezed Miriam's shoulder in a side hug before shaking Shawn's hand.

"Okay, now that we have the pleasantries out of the way, how about I help you all to your rooms."

"You? You know you're not climbing those stairs. You mean Rosa?" Julie Ann leaned her head towards her husband with a knowing look.

He smiled and kissed her on her forehead. "You're right. How about Rosa show you all to your rooms. And then you all come back down, and we can cover the agenda for the weekend. I'm not sure if you're hungry, but I did have my chef prepare food for you all. It's late in the evening, but I don't know if it's too late for you youngsters to hang out on the back deck for cocktails. The Mrs. and I have already eaten and plan to retire not too long after the drinks and a little conversation when you all come back down."

"Okay," Miriam said.

Shawn merely nodded.

"Follow me," Rosa said and attempted to take as many of Shawn and Miriam's belongings as she could, but Shawn smiled at her and quickly grabbed the bags from her.

Mr. Schaeffer turned his back to them and began making his way towards his office, but Shawn's voice stalled his footsteps. "Mr. Schaeffer, can I speak to you for a moment?"

"Sure." Ready to hear him out, he took steps back towards Shawn.

"In private?"

"Okay, then. Since I see that vice grip of yours is refusing to allow Rosa to take those bags from you, I'll let her show you to your room." He turned to Rosa. "Escort him to my study afterward, please."

She nodded her head and started for the stairs, bag free since Shawn refused to let her do her job and carry the bags to their rooms. She didn't know the pair of visitors, but she found herself laughing inwardly at them, observing the way Shawn stared at Miriam and how after an intense stare between them, Miriam refused to look in Shawn's direction again.

Rosa may not have known much about the pair, but she knew chemistry when she saw it.

After making it to the third floor, Rosa pointed to the first bedroom to the left. "Ms. Caldwell, you'll be staying here." She opened the door to a massive bedroom with a queen-sized bed centering a wall and a beautiful view of the waters and the beach shore.

"Thank you." Miriam smiled and had almost stepped in the room, but Rosa's voice paused her.

"And Mr. Lafayette, you'll be staying here."

Please let him be across the hall. Or even on another floor.

She peeked her head out and to her disappointment, saw Shawn cross the threshold of the room directly next to hers.

Really not wanting to sleep so close to him, she whispered, "Rosa. Rosa."

"Yes?" Rosa soon joined Miriam in her bedroom.

"Is there another bedroom I can stay in? Across the hall? Or even better, on another floor?"

Miriam's hushed tone, the way she leaned in to talk to Rosa and the desperate look on her face, pressured Rosa to laugh out loud, but she couldn't dare behave like that in front of guests. Realizing Miriam didn't want Shawn privy to their conversation, she leaned into her and whispered as well. She also felt like she understood what Miriam was asking her. She'd read her uptight body language. "I can, but the other bedrooms haven't been prepared for visitors, so it will take me some time to get another one ready."

Miriam didn't want to impose her issues on to Rosa. "Never mind. This room will do just fine. Thank you." She closed the door behind Rosa after she left out.

She could hear the conversation in the hallway and as usual, his voice always managed to make her heart skip beats, her breathing labor.

"Are you ready to see Mr. Schaeffer?"

"Yes, just give me a second."

She decided to use the time Shawn would speak with Mr. Schaeffer, although she was curious to know what he wanted to discuss with him, to freshen up for dinner and hopefully talk her body into not reacting to Shawn whenever he was around.

The weekend would force her to encounter him more than she ever had before. If their kiss, his knee bumping against hers on the plane was any indication of how it was to be around him constantly, then she needed prayer and a lot of it.

She grabbed her toiletry bag from her purse and headed to the en-suite bathroom door that Rosa had pointed out to her. She pulled the door open and her eyes bulged, and her breath caught in her throat as she stared at a shirtless Shawn brushing his teeth. She knew her kisser had a nice body when her hand scaled his chest in search of his face, but her quick touches didn't capture what was really beneath his shirt.

The man was ripped.

He couldn't have anybody fat the way his smooth dark chestnut skin clung to his muscles. Every inch her eyes landed on made her mouth water.

He paused when he looked up at her, but the contracting of his muscles had already made her core wet.

He quickly rinsed his mouth and grabbed a towel on the door behind her, causing her to get a deep inhale of his scent. She closed her eyes, willing all the naughty thoughts trying to take residence in her brain to go away, but images of him were still too vivid, so she opened her eyes as his arm slowly withdrew from behind her.

"I'm sorry. I wanted to freshen up before I head downstairs. I'm done brushing my teeth, but I needed to grab a towel and the only one I saw was behind you." His voice was low as he towered her and stared into her hazel eyes.

"Uh." At a loss for words, she pivoted on her heels as she raced out of the Jack and Jill bathroom and closed the door behind her.

She fell back on the tall bed behind her, but quickly covered her face with a pillow to scream in it. *Maybe running from him just then wasn't the maturest way I've behaved in life, but I could tell by the look in his eyes he knows how he affects my body.* "Ahhh!" she screamed again into the pillow.

***

"Just knock. He's in there." Rosa smiled at Shawn before walking away.

Shawn nodded his head at her and then tapped on the door.

"Come in, Shawn." Mr. Schaeffer looked up at Shawn entering with a pinched expression. "No need to be nervous about whatever it is you have to ask or say. Just get it out."

Shawn went and stood in front of his desk and braced his hands in the pockets of his jeans.

"Sit," Mr. Schaeffer said in an inviting voice.

"Okay." Shawn sat and relaxed somewhat as Mr. Schaeffer sat back in his worn leather office chair. "Well sir, Miriam and I are in more than competition for hotel designs and a promotion."

A wry smile crept on Mr. Schaeffer's face, which was similar to the distressed look of the leather he sat on, but his skin lacked the rich, brown hues. He was pale, except for the myriad of age spots freckling his face. "I knew it." He let out a hearty laugh, and his gut stretched out his polo shirt more than what seemed possible. "I just knew from the way you looked at her, versus the way she avoided looking at you, that something was going on between you two. How long have you been dating? Find it hard to compete against the woman you love for a job?" Mr. Schaeffer sat upright in his seat and narrowed his eyes in on Shawn.

Love? Is that how I looked at her. He shook his head, trying to erase the absurdity of what Mr. Schaeffer had said. He would readily admit that he liked Miriam, had a strong attraction to her that went beyond just like, but love her? *How could that be when the woman barely says anything to me?* He focused his eyesight to see Mr. Schaeffer staring at him. He decided to put any misunderstandings to rest. "Sir, Miriam and I aren't dating, just yet. So, love is not even in the equation."

Mr. Schaeffer pressed his lips tightly together.

"You see, sir, we both somehow ended up on a game show where we kissed strangers in blindfolds."

Mr. Schaeffer's eyebrows furrowed.

"Unconventional I know, sir, but the show's premise was to see if people could really find love at first kiss."

"And did you?" Mr. Schaeffer smirked.

Shawn paused, contemplating that word *love* again and if that was what he really felt for Miriam. "I haven't thought about that much yet but kissing her that night was the greatest moment I've experienced in my life."

Mr. Schaeffer smiled. "So, what's the hold up between you two? I could gather from your interactions at the door alone that she was just as attracted to you as you are to her."

"She doesn't believe in work romances. And she doesn't want to focus on anything else but getting the promotion."

Mr. Schaeffer merely nodded his head.

Shawn didn't know what to make of Mr. Schaeffer's silence. He figured it'd be best if he got straight to the point. "I received a call from the producer of the show right before I left from work today and headed here. He went on about how obvious the attraction was between Miriam and I as we kissed on camera. In fact, they had to make sirens go off and pull us apart to make us stop." A genuine smile planted itself on Shawn's face as he paused for a second, briefly recounting the kiss.

Mr. Schaeffer looked at him knowing a truth Shawn hadn't yet admitted to himself.

"They want to interview us again so that when the kiss airs, they can show our lives after the kiss, but there hasn't been an *us* since the kiss. She doesn't want anything to do with me, and I'm certain that she won't do the taping. However, I want to do it as a way to corner her and talk about an *us*."

Mr. Schaeffer smiled, noting the desperation in Shawn's voice. "How am I supposed to help you?"

Shawn perked up. "The producer informed me that they're taping here in Charleston this weekend and would love to interview us. When you mentioned having an agenda for us to follow this weekend, it made me dare to ask if you'd put the studio visit on the itineraries you give us? She'd have no choice but to show up there." He added the last of his statement for good measure.

"So, you want me to amend the agenda and put what on there, Post Kiss Interview?"

Shawn stood up, unsure if trying to solicit help from the man whose decision could finally give him what he wanted, career-wise, was the best move after all. "I'm sorry to waste your time, sir." Shawn turned to walk to the door, but the amusement in Mr. Schaeffer's voice when he called his name confused him and made him turn back to face the business mogul.

Mr. Schaeffer laughed out loud as he picked up his phone and dialed his personal assistant's number. She picked up on the third ring. "Sorry to bother you, Sylvia. I know you already left the printed agendas here for me on my desk, but I need you to make a change to it…No, no, no. You didn't do anything wrong, there's just a last-minute item I need you to add to Sunday morning before we convene at the house and I announce whose design I'll choose."

Shawn stood up straighter at the mention of the announcement. He had been putting so much mental focus into Miriam that he slipped in and out of awareness of the pending promotion. He shifted his body weight from one foot to the other, hoping that by Sunday evening he'd have the job and the woman.

"No, you don't have to bring it here. You're way across town. I can manage to open up my email and print it." He chuckled. "Thank you and enjoy the rest of your evening." He hung up the phone and looked up at Shawn, who seemed to be holding his breath. "You happy now?"

Shawn wasn't sure if his question was sarcastic or sincere. He didn't want his answer to shift Mr. Schaeffer's seemingly jovial mood, so he pasted a smile on his face as he nodded.

Mr. Schaeffer clicked the mouse on his desk. "It's okay. I admire a man who will go the distance to get what he wants. And I can tell from the tension between you two when you first came in that there's something special between you two. Realized or not, there's something there." He was up out of his seat and headed to the printer by the time he finished the last of his statement.

He looked over the agendas before he walked back

to his desk and switched them out with the old agendas in the Manila folders.

He rounded his desk and went and stood next to Shawn and braced a firm hand on his shoulder. "Whaduya say we go have a few drinks? I'm certain while I'm studying you two, you'll probably be studying her." He laughed hard as he walked ahead of Shawn.

***

Shawn stepped out onto the dimly lit deck, and his breath caught in his throat as his eyes roamed Miriam's exposed long and sexy legs all the way up to her face.

He watched her with her head back, mouth open and laughing incessantly with Mrs. Schaeffer. He'd never seen her smile that wide or her eyes so bright and it pulled at another piece of his heart. Over the years, he hated not knowing much about her and yet sensed there was so much treasure to discover about her.

Her laugh. Her smile said a lot about her at the moment. With the ease with which she rested her hand on Mrs. Schaeffer's arm as she continued to laugh, he just knew how lively she could be when she let her guard down. He was even more determined to get her to see she could be that way with him.

He took a step forward, and her head turned towards him. Their eyes locked, and her eyes dimmed in apprehension. He hated that he couldn't continue to simply take her in. He wouldn't rest until he removed the look of doubt in her eyes where he was concerned.

"Come join us," Mr. Schaeffer said, laughing.

Still holding Miriam's gaze and cherishing it, Shawn walked closer to the trio, but Mr. Schaeffer's voice quickly pulled her eyes away from him.

Wine glasses were already filled, and Mr. Schaeffer directed everyone to hold their glasses high. He paused and looked at Miriam. "You won't drink with us?"

"No, sir. I just want to be focused on this weekend."

Mr. Schaeffer laughed. "Nonsense Miriam. It's one thing if you aren't a drinker, I can respect that. But don't be afraid to be yourself in front of me if you are."

She wouldn't dare bring up her mother's addiction to any of them, but she also wouldn't compromise on the promise she made to herself to never drink.

Sensing her uneasiness, Shawn spoke up. "If it's alright with you, sir, Miriam and I can just have water for the toast." Shawn looked over and smiled at her.

There was a quick glance of gratitude she cast his way before she swiftly turned away from him and fidgeted with her hands in her lap.

Shawn scooted to the end of his seat, poured Miriam and himself glasses of water from the chilled pitcher on the table in front of them, and handed her a glass. Her hand accidentally locked around his as she tried to take the glass from him.

That same bolt of fiery energy he felt when they

kissed, and every time he saw or thought of her, coursed through his body. He knew she felt it too with how stiff her body became in her seat. He felt her hand trembling as it covered his and she bit her bottom lip, which he reasoned must be a nervous response of hers.

Staring at her biting her full, what he knew to be kissable lip, only made him want to take over the action for her. He could feel himself slowly leaning forward ready to command her lips and tongue to yield to the desire brewing between them, but the sound of Mr. Schaeffer clearing his throat reminded him that they weren't alone.

She pulled her hand away from his and pushed her glasses up on her face, trying to recompose herself.

Shawn instantly missed her touch and staring into her eyes.

"You know what, darling, I say we call it a night." Mr. Schaeffer stood and reached out his hand to help his smirking wife stand.

"I think so too," Mrs. Schaeffer said, now standing next to her husband.

"The agendas for the weekend are in the folder." He pointed to the Manila folders on the table mere inches away from the water pitcher. "It's simple to follow along, but if you have any questions regarding it, feel free to ask before we play tennis in the morning.

"Not sure if either of you are early birds or late to rise, so I didn't set a formal breakfast time, but Rosa will be in the kitchen at 5 a.m., ready to fill your requests. Good night you all," Mr. Schaeffer said, and then he and his wife walked hand in hand back into the house.

Shawn and Miriam reached for their folders at the same time, but not wanting her body to react to his touch the way it did moments earlier, she acquiesced to him grabbing one first.

"No, you can have the first look," he said in a low and steady voice as he stared at her.

Any other time, she may have gone back and forth with him about not needing him to offer her anything, but she needed to get away from him as soon as possible. Away from his stare. Away from eyes that told exactly how he felt about her.

"Thank you," was all she managed to say through parched lips as she grabbed her agenda and rushed to the door.

Shawn had skimmed the agenda by the time she made it to the door and yelled out, "See you on the tennis court in the morning if I don't see you downstairs for breakfast before then." He smiled as he watched her pause at the door before she took off even faster than she had when she vacated her seat seconds ago.

Miriam made it up to her room as quickly as she could and locked the door behind her. Never before had a man made her heart race, her palms sweaty, her mouth dry, her spine tingle, and her core as wet as Shawn Lafayette did. And that was when she wasn't kissing him.

She hated that he had that kind of effect on her. She only wanted to be concerned with the upward advancement of her career. Not only had Shawn made her acutely aware that she was a woman with desires that had been long unfulfilled, but that he stood in the way of the something she could use to prove to her mother that she was someone special indeed.

She walked over to the chair near the window and took a seat. The night's gentle summer breeze accompanied her as she read the agenda aloud. "Tennis with Mr. and Mrs. Schaeffer at ten, tour the site of the first hotel to be redesigned, and then dinner on his boat at night."

Sighing, she grabbed her luggage, opened it and retrieved her toiletries to shower, realizing that every moment of the next day seemed to somehow involve time spent with Shawn. Clearly, there would be no reprieve for her body or her nerve endings from him.

Shawn made it to his room. He wanted to shower and look over his proposal, but the sound of water running let him know that Miriam had beaten him to his first idea.

The thought of her naked on the other side of the bathroom door he stared at magnetized his feet to it. He dropped his head against the door in frustration, but more so, in wonder of how she looked on the other side of the door.

He was envious of the water he was certain was running down her back whereas he wished it were his tongue and lips bathing her in kisses from her feet to her head. He wanted to lightly trace his fingers over the small tattoo on her shoulder her tank top exposed when they were downstairs for drinks with the Schaeffers. He never would've pegged her for the type to have a tattoo, but it was beautiful against her almond skin, and he couldn't wait for her to open up to him and share the story behind the eagle adorning her skin.

Fearing he might turn the knob and walk in if he stood there any longer, he put distance between himself and the door. He flopped down on the bed and looked at the agenda he still clutched in his hand.

He was sure Saturday's succession of events would position him to learn more about Miriam, give her the chance to see he wasn't the bad guy she must've thought he was, but it was the first thing after breakfast Sunday that most excited him.

They would go to the studio, and if she hadn't caved to him by Saturday night, he would do all he could, as he knew the producer would too, to get Miriam to see they belonged together.

The water stopped running in the bathroom, and Shawn stilled himself as he listened for the next thing she would do. The bulge in his pants strained against his jeans and it reminded him of his fantasies of her.

He wondered what she would wear to bed that night. He'd only seen her in baggy clothes at work, but clearly, there was a different side to her, because the royal blue and short shorts she had on when he stepped onto the patio gave him a full, luxurious view of her long, smooth legs. And the way she walked away from him after the Schaeffer's left gave him a great view of her ample butt.

He heard the door to her room from the bathroom close and hated the additional distance the bathroom put between them.

Maybe a shower would do him some good. Rid his mind of images of a naked Miriam and free his thoughts to look over his proposal once more.

Sexually frustrated, he snatched his shirt off and sped into the bathroom.

Miriam had just finished lathering body oil on her legs when she heard the shower running. The image of water cascading down Shawn's ripped abs popped in her head and her core tingled.

She shook her head in protest of her line of thinking.

She grabbed the fuchsia pajama short set that she had laid out to sleep in and slipped it on. She got her laptop and powered it on. Looking at architectural structures always centered her. She planned to look through the many photos she found of the buildings to be renovated and imagined her designs to transform them.

She was staring at picture number two when Shawn's deep, yet off-key sounding voice reached her ears from beyond the bathroom door. He was singing a slow tune. "Every time I see yo' face it makes me wanna sing, and every time I think about your love it drives me crazy. I belong to you…"

She fell back on the bed and covered her face and ears with a plush pillow trying to drown out the sound of his voice, but it only seemed to get louder. She found herself smiling against the pillow and knew it would be of no use to her. She threw it at the bathroom door and sighed.

She wanted to focus on work, but Shawn's singing had shifted her thoughts back on him. *Is he dancing while he sings? Has he dried off yet or are there soap bubbles still caressing his taut, dark skin?*

She couldn't afford to keep thinking about him the way she was.

She jumped up out of her bed, rushed to the bathroom door, and banged on it as she shouted his name, "Shawn. Shawn."

The water stopped running, and she heard a commotion behind the door before it flung open and the view answered one of her questions. He indeed still had soap clinging to his chiseled chest. Suds slowly slid down his sculpted arms.

"Yes, Miriam?" He panted as he struggled to hold the towel securely around his waist. "You okay? Is everything alright in here?" He craned his neck in the room for any signs of the danger that had her banging on the door as if she needed him to come to her rescue.

Her mouth was dry, and she couldn't manage to focus her eyes above his neck. The sight in front of her was magnificent. The water intensified the sight of just how fit he was. He offered much for her to take in visually. Her core moistened even more so than when his hand had touched hers earlier.

The sound of panic in his voice when calling her name let her know that he would have no qualms battling whoever may have been offending her and put her in need of his help.

That heartfelt epiphany is what helped her to refocus her attention to his face, and when they locked eyes, Miriam knew she had to get him out the room, quick. And out of her head. Maybe even out of her heart.

"Mimi, are you okay?" The possessive gaze he had trained on her softened as he questioned her.

"Yes." She found her voice. "You were just so loud, and I was trying to get some sleep." She rubbed her neck and tried to look anywhere but at the white towel resting on his hips.

Shawn looked over to her bed. "So you fall asleep with your laptop too?" he asked with one brow raised.

"Hunh?" She followed his eyes to her bed to see her

bright laptop screen. "Oh, yes." She looked back at him to see his eyes slowly roaming her body. She finally inhaled the ocean breeze scent of his body wash and her nipples hardened. He must've noticed the bud's tightening too as he licked his lips.

The desire in his eyes made her core pulse, and she imagined what he would do to her if she only gave him clearance to have his way with her.

Still not comfortable with the idea of them, she instinctively folded her arms across her chest to somehow shield herself from his penetrating stare and realized she didn't have a bra on.

Wanting more than for her to stand there bashfully avoiding him, Shawn took a step towards her, but Miriam held up her hand in protest.

"Good night, Shawn," she said with a bit of hesitancy in her voice. "Please close the door behind you."

Shawn stared at her as she walked out on the balcony of her room. He wasn't sure how much longer he'd take heed to her pushing him away, but he obliged her for the night.

Miriam let out the breath she was holding when she heard the door softly close. It took everything in her to push Shawn away.

She knew it just had to be her hormones egging her to give in to him. Not the good sense she had to know that she *had* to accomplish getting promoted before she would even consider delving into a romantic relationship. And even still, she knew it couldn't be with Shawn.

She didn't have much experience in the love department, but she felt she knew enough to know that work romances weren't for her. For one, having purposely kept to herself all the years at her firm, she didn't know how, and if, she'd be able to handle all the gossip and stares attached to dating someone like Shawn.

What if she got the promotion? How would he take her being his boss? Even worse, how could she handle it if he got the promotion?

She shuddered at the thought of loving a man she lost her most sought-after goal to. She knew she had to continue to ignore the way her body reacted to him, the way her heart fluttered when he looked at her with admiration.

She went back into the room, peeled the covers back and tried to relax in the soft bed, but sleep evaded her. All she could think of was how scrumptious he looked with suds covering his exposed skin.

She squeezed her thigh muscles tighter and tried to find sleep instead of witnessing the vivid mental images of Shawn's towel-covered body on top of hers.

19

"I thought you said you could play tennis, Shawn? We're losing and not by a few points. They are kicking our butts," Mr. Schaeffer chided Shawn as he readied his stance for his wife's serve across the court.

"I'm sorry, sir. I can, but I just can't seem to focus right now."

Mr. Schaeffer grinned as he looked at Shawn out the corner of his eye. "I can tell. You're too busy looking at her legs instead of the ball."

Shawn stood straight up and stared at Mr. Schaeffer. "Is it that obvious, sir?"

Mr. Schaeffer chuckled. "Indeed, it is."

"Sorry sir, but we can still win this game if we work together."

"You really haven't been paying attention. One more point for them and this game is over."

"For real?" Shawn's eyebrows furrowed.

Mr. Schaeffer grunted and went chasing after the ball, but he was too late. It hit the ground before his racquet could touch it.

Excited they had won their game, Mrs. Schaeffer and Miriam high-fived each other. They made their way to center court as did Shawn and Mr. Schaeffer.

Mr. Schaeffer panted as he leaned across the net to kiss his wife, Julie Ann. "Good game. You looked so youthful out there."

She smiled and twirled in her white, pleated skirt and ended her celebration with a curtsy. "Even though you're out of breath, we still have to play one more game. I want to stay looking young and you know tennis is my Saturday morning workout."

"I can go another round after I catch my breath, but what I can't do is lose again. You know I hate losing." He looked over at Shawn. "So Shawn, I'm playing with my wife and you can partner up with Miriam."

After Mr. Schaeffer's declaration, Shawn didn't miss Miriam's slight snarl that transformed into a tight smile.

He knew she didn't want to have much to do with him, but he couldn't be bothered with her doubts at the moment, everything about her captivated him.

He had made it down to breakfast to see her sitting at the kitchen table and the only thing he could focus on was her thick almond colored thigh peeking at him. It made him jealous of the gray shorts she was wearing and how they clung to her skin. He'd prefer it be his body molded to hers.

She caught him staring at her, but it didn't bother him because the hesitant look in her eyes gave him hope before she dashed out of the kitchen.

The way her shorts hugged her, the way her fitted tank top revealed just how perky her breasts were, and the way she managed to constantly push her glasses up the bridge of her nose in between hitting killer shots, affected his ability to play the game.

He jumped over the net and walked closer to her. For a second, he thought maybe playing next to her would force his attention on the game and not her, but one scintillating whiff of her perfume and he knew it wouldn't matter whether she was in front of him or next to him, she consumed his thoughts. Maybe even his heart.

Trying to get control of himself and maybe throw her off the way she affected him, he walked and stood mere inches away from her, towered over her, and said, "You ready to do this, partner?" He knew she couldn't mistake the longing in his voice when she gazed into his eyes before stepping back and clearing her throat.

"Let's just get this over with," she said, barely audible and rubbing her neck.

He smiled as she walked away.

Mr. Schaeffer chuckled at the exchange between them and he and his wife made their way to the other side of the net.

As they walked back to their places on the court to prepare for the next game, Miriam turned her head and looked over at Shawn and said, "You better not lose this game."

The command was the sexiest thing Shawn had ever heard her say. It was just what he needed to kick him into high gear and help her kick the Schaeffer's' butts.

Although he was highly competitive and could tell she was too, he didn't play as aggressive as he could have. He let her do most of the work. Watching her lunge forward and run from side to side, trying to keep the ball from hitting the ground gave him a great viewpoint of her body. He did just enough to keep them in the lead.

Thirty minutes later, she was drenched in sweat and pleased with his performance. She stood wiping sweat from her forehead and bare arms when Shawn walked up to her.

He held his hand up to high-five her with a sexy smirk on his face. "Good job, partner."

Miriam couldn't bring herself to look at him. The sudden breeze blew his scent her way. She didn't understand how someone covered in sweat could still smell as good as he did.

His scent intoxicated her and made her imagine things that she didn't want to about him.

Not wanting to let the moment of pointing out to her that they made a great team pass, he stepped closer to her before he said, "We make a great team, don't we?"

"What do you think?" She still refused to look at him.

He stepped even closer to her and rubbed the back of his hand against her arm. "Do you really want me to respond to you, Mimi?" He looked down at her.

Miriam's throat was suddenly dry. It was as if the sun's temperature rose. His penetrating stare had become too much for her. She stepped back from him, stuttering, trying to find the right words to say. "I, um…"

Luckily for her, Mr. Schaeffer and his wife approached them, and Miriam found it easy to think again.

"I guess you aren't a bad player after all." Mr. Schaeffer grinned as he stared at Shawn and Miriam. He would never out him, and he felt bad that Miriam didn't know just how much Shawn liked her, but he couldn't help but laugh at the struggle between the duo.

He could clearly see Shawn trying to pull her in, while she was working at all costs to ignore the obvious chemistry between the two of them.

Shawn finally pulled his stare from Miriam to address Mr. Schaeffer and she silently thanked God for the reprieve.

He smiled at Mr. Schaeffer. "I told you I wasn't."

"Alright, no gloating." Mr. Schaeffer chuckled. "Let's head back to the house. We need to clean up and get over to the hotel for a tour." Mr. Schaeffer allowed his wife to walk in front of him as they headed out of the gated court, but he smacked her on the butt before she made it past the gate.

She winked, looking back at him.

Shawn extended his hand to let Miriam walk in front of him, but she shook her head and said, "There will be no monkey see, monkey do with me."

Shawn could only laugh as he held his hands up in defense. "I would never do such a thing…yet," he mumbled the latter part to himself. "I'm just being a gentleman and let a lady walk ahead of me. I'll even stay back ten paces from you. Go ahead." He nodded at her and she reluctantly walked ahead of him.

He counted aloud, "One, two, three…" He chuckled as he continued to count and didn't move his feet to follow behind her until he reached the number ten.

ANITA DAVIS

20

Miriam walked into the hotel first with a bright smile on her face.

Shawn's facial expression was less telling. And not because he wasn't as enthusiastic about seeing one of the many hotels he would be responsible for reconstructing, but because in his opinion, the view of Miriam's backside was far more appealing, more breathtaking than any wooden, cement, or steel structure he could ever create.

He didn't dare reduce her to only her physical beauty, but given their infrequency of talking, he was left mostly to just visually explore her curves, the deep dimple in her left cheek. Man did he want to lick it.

"Shawn. Shawn," Mr. Schaeffer called out to him from several paces ahead. "You plan on keeping up with us?"

"Uh, yes, sir." Shawn took a light jog and caught

up to Mr. Schaeffer and Miriam in no time.

Miriam's breathing shifted when he fell in stride next to her.

"As I was saying, Mr. Schaeffer, there are several ways in which we could proceed with this particular hotel's design. Although I haven't fully inspected it yet, I say that we can keep much of the structure standing as is, but by the time we're done with the amendments and additions, no one would be wise to the fact we actually didn't start from the ground up." Her smile was wide. "Talk about southern charm, I could absolutely see an atrium right next to the pool in the center of the hotel. And not just any old atrium, we could have flowers indigenous of mostly every country from around the world. Make people feel like they've visited a thousand places by the end of their stay here."

"I like your thinking, Miriam," Mr. Schaeffer said as he looked at her.

Shawn marveled at the light in Miriam's eyes as she spoke of her designs. He loved hearing her voice and didn't want to rain on her parade, but he had to assert himself at that point. "Well sir, in my opinion, I say it'd be best to tear this building down and start from scratch. I've stayed in enough hotels with pools in the center of the rooms to know that it's really not a fan favorite.

"Even with central air, it can get muggy in here with a centered indoor pool. I think out-of-towners would enjoy soaking up the sun poolside. If we want the hotel to appeal to all kinds of travelers, we have to keep that in mind with the design."

Bearing in mind that Mr. Schaeffer was present, Miriam pursed her lips to keep from talking. Otherwise, her response to Shawn cutting her off wouldn't have been as hushed as she was forcing herself to be.

"I see your point as well, Shawn," Mr. Schaeffer said with his back to Shawn as he kicked at the baseboard of a wall as if detecting its durability solely from the method.

Miriam took the opportunity to shoot Shawn a disapproving look.

He pretended to ignore her vicious stare.

They continued walking the site, each sharing snippets of their ideas, battling as to how they would redo the space.

Shawn ignored every menacing stare Miriam aimed at him. When she wasn't looking at him with disdain, he smiled at her, taking in how beautiful she was as she shared her design ideas.

The woman was simply stunning, mad or not. He didn't know who to thank for her sudden change of attire. Since they'd gotten there, her fitted clothes, in contrast to the baggy ones she wore to work all the time, gave him the perfect view of her luscious body.

They finally made it to the rooftop. Mr. Schaeffer caught his breath as if they took all twenty flights of stairs there as opposed to riding the elevator.

Shawn raised one eyebrow at him. "You okay, sir?"

Mr. Schaeffer laughed. "I'll be fine once my breathing returns to normal. When you get my age, the simplest of things become more tasking."

"Your age? You can't be more than fifty-five, sir," Miriam said grinning, walking closer to him.

He stood up straight and puffed his chest out. "Fifty-five, try adding a little over ten years to that."

"I don't believe you." She smiled wider.

"No, sir. I'm with Miriam. I'll give you fifty-seven tops," Shawn said, walking closer to the duo.

Miriam took a deep breath smelling his sexy cologne versus being annoyed that he had once again taken over the conversation.

How could one man tap into so many of her emotions at one time?

"I'm in my late sixties you two and that's the honest truth. My age is also why I need to see this hotel chain flourish. I'm late getting in the hospitality industry, but I know I have enough left in me to really make this thing grow and leave more of a legacy for my children and their children."

"With how successful you are with your other businesses, sir, I'm certain that you've made them proud several times over," Miriam said as she finally put on her sunglasses to shield her eyes from the sun's glare.

Shawn cursed under his breath. He wanted to keep looking into her hazel eyes for as long as possible, but the sunglasses thwarted that desire for the time being.

He redirected his attention to Mr. Schaeffer. "Why just the other day, I was reading up on the article of you in Time magazine's top ten business moguls. It did a good job of highlighting your successes. Listed your net worth. Sir, you've done more than well for yourself, for your family."

"Yes, I enjoyed that interview. One in which they didn't try to dig for any negative stuff on me or my family. Those are always the best ones." Mr. Schaeffer smiled and patted Shawn's back.

Miriam bit her tongue. Since they'd been on the tour, Shawn had managed to have the last say on topics that she brought up. It looked to her as if Mr. Schaeffer was favoring him more than her. A thought hit her. "Mr.—"

"Mr. Schaeffer," Shawn said as an idea had taken hold of him as well, "I think it'd be perfect if we created a rooftop atmosphere. I'm thinking pool, cabanas, bars. Not only would it be great for guests staying here, but you could also rent it out for private parties." His steps followed Mr. Schaeffer's over to the perimeter of the roof. "And if we go with my design of tearing the place down and starting from scratch, we can build it so that there's a stage for small performances. Make it a place that people near and far will want to frequent..." Shawn continued sharing his renovation ideas with Mr. Schaeffer, and it seemed as if the chubby old man was eating up every idea shared.

Miriam's nostrils flared as she stood by trying to edge her way in the conversation, but she just couldn't find the proper room to speak.

"Well, sir—" she finally opened her mouth to share some more of her ideas, but Mr. Schaeffer's heavy voice cut her off.

"My hip's buzzing and I see that it's the Mrs. I heard what both of you said and I look forward to going over each of your proposals, but I think it's time to make our way back to the house." He walked ahead of them.

Shawn's head turned until his eyes landed on a seemingly flustered Miriam. He took steps towards her, but she turned and quickened her steps to catch up with Mr. Schaeffer.

Shawn took slow steps and watched her shapely legs practically skip off the rooftop. From the look of disdain on her face when he prepped to near her, she seemed upset with him. It made him wonder what he did to push her farther away from him.

21

The sun was on its last leg before it would finally set, and the boat swayed with just enough force to feel the waves but not make those onboard nauseous.

Shawn kept a comfortable distance between himself and Miriam since it gave him a full view of her beauty. He loved the way the plum fitted dress melted against her body, but since his interest in her was more than physical, he planned on using their time on the boat to get her to see him in a different light. He needed her to see that he was a cool guy and that there was no need to fear romance happening between them.

Hearing the blond-haired woman Miriam was conversing with say she had to run to the bathroom, Shawn found himself walking towards her to seize the opportunity to get her alone. She turned her head to see his advancing steps towards her and rushed off to join a trio of women in what seemed to be a deep conversation.

He tried several more times over the next hour to get her alone to talk to her, but she always evaded him by joining another discussion before he could engage her.

Wanting her to himself, he either pretended to pay attention to others onboard who called him into their discussion or just stood off by himself, quietly admiring her.

He noticed a lot about her in that hour. He didn't know exactly what she was saying in each conversation, but he gathered a lot about her from her body language. She held her head up high and made direct eye contact when talking in the groups, which meant to him, her whole quiet act around the office was just a means to keep distance between herself and her coworkers. What gnawed at him about that was the *why* she was so standoffish?

In his opinion, no woman at the firm could hold a candle to her when it came to beauty, and since she was his competition for the promotion, obviously no one else could compare to her in brains, well except for him. He chuckled at the thought of her being his equal. Not a chuckle like it was absurd to think she could be as smart as him, but a chuckle of relief like he'd finally found her. His match.

"I'm sorry, did I say something funny?" the short man to the left of the table asked Shawn.

"No. I don't think so. I'm sorry, my mind drifted

off for a second." Shawn sat upright in his seat, preparing to focus his attention back to Mr. Schaeffer and the other two gentlemen sitting at the table.

"Where to, Miriam?" the short man asked in jest and they all chuckled, all except for Shawn.

Shawn's eyebrows furrowed in confusion.

"No need to be confused about how they know. You told me so yourself, but these two picked up on your attraction for her instantly. You haven't contributed a single thought to this conversation, and they've followed your line of vision to her across this boat all night," Mr. Schaeffer said, gripping his glass of bourbon and smirking.

"Sorry, gentlemen."

"You don't seem like the type to shy away from a woman, Shawn," the short man said.

"I'm not. It's just that I've tried with her, but she won't budge on giving us a chance."

"So how are you going to convince her to give you a chance then?" the bald one asked.

"I'm working on that, but it's going to happen." Shawn sat back in his seat as the other men at the table shared stories of how they snagged their wives. He scanned the boat until he laid eyes on her again.

He had noticed during their time on the boat that when she wasn't exuding confidence in her posture talking to others, it was because they had locked eyes intermittently only to have her look away and then rub her neck or fold her arms tightly across her chest. It was as if she was trying to guard herself from him.

Guessing his stare made her uncomfortable, he continued to keep it on her. He wanted her to know he was watching her and that she had an effect on him too. That and the fact that he loved looking at her with her hair free from its usual bun.

Miriam hadn't taken a vacation the entire time she worked at the firm. Being out on the boat, with the soft breeze hitting her, was making her see that she indeed needed to take some time for herself soon. Of course, after she secured her promotion and settled into the role.

She excused herself from the group she was chatting with and walked over to an empty spot on the deck to enjoy the dark skies, alone.

Shawn's eyes followed her to her new spot. She was so beautiful, especially with her eyes closed and relaxed against the waist-high rail. Apparently, she was too relaxed. Reaching up as if she could touch the stars twinkling in the sky, she lost her footing and fell overboard.

"Miriam," Shawn belted out and dashed from his seat to the spot where she had just stood. His actions had drawn others attention to him and by that point had amassed the small crowd onboard around him.

"Miriam," he leaned over the rail, calling out in search of her.

With arms flailing, her head surfaced just above the

water and she screamed, "Help. Help."

Shawn didn't think twice about jumping in to save her. He braced his hands on the rail and used them to propel him over it as he dived into the water. "Miriam, it's okay. I got you."

Crying, eyes closed, and mouth still filling with water, she continued flailing her arms and screaming, "Help me. I can't swim." The fear of drowning overwhelmed her, and she continued to struggle in Shawn's arms until he lifted her up and cradled her body close to his.

He whispered coolly in her ear, "Relax. I promise I have you."

There was something about the reassurance in his deep voice that calmed her. She wrapped her arms around his neck, stilled her body, and laid her head on his shoulder.

Shawn waded over to the stairs connected to the boat and took them one by one until he was back on the deck.

"Is she alright?" Mr. Schaeffer's wife asked as she braced her hand on Miriam's back.

"I think so. Just probably shook up from the ordeal," Shawn said, looking down at Miriam who was shivering in his arms.

"Come on, Miriam, let's get you cleaned up." Mrs. Schaeffer tried to pull on Miriam to go with her, but she squeezed Shawn's neck harder and buried her head deeper into his chest.

He gripped her tighter to him and said, "Just show me the way, Mrs. Schaeffer."

Mr. Schaeffer tried to return the atmosphere to some type of normalcy for the others on board as he ordered the server to refresh everyone's drinks.

Mrs. Schaeffer led them down the stairs into a bedroom. She opened the door and turned back toward them. "Shawn, just take her in there and I'll help her get changed."

When Mrs. Schaeffer cleared the doorway, Shawn ducked his head and stepped into the bedroom. "Miriam, I'm going to put you down on the bed, okay?"

Mrs. Schaeffer busied herself rummaging through dresser drawers, looking for towels and clothes that might fit either of them

Miriam, still shivering, clung even closer to him and pressed her forehead tighter to his chest as he bent over trying to place her on the bed. "Okay." He stood up as best as he could in the small space with her still in his arms. He looked back at Mrs. Schaeffer. "I'll just stay with her for a bit then come out and get you."

"Okay." She laid what she had found on the foot of the bed and left out.

"Miriam?" Shawn said with his chin in his chest, trying to look at her. "You okay? We gotta get you out of these wet clothes now. That may stop you from shivering." He unhooked his left arm from the crooks of her knees and bent over trying to get her to stand, but she rotated her body so that she locked her legs around his waist with her arms tightly around his neck and her head buried between the two of them.

Shawn had to take a deep breath and quell the desire he had for her. Many nights he laid awake in bed, imagining her legs wrapped around his waist as she lay naked underneath him and he forged deeper and deeper into her with each stroke.

Knowing then was not the time to dwell on that fantasy or try to make it a reality, he quietly chastised himself.

He gently ran his hand up and down her back. "Miriam, you're still shivering, and your teeth are chattering. You have to get out of these wet clothes. So do I." He lowered his hands to her waist and then his hands slowly glided along her thighs.

Applying gentle pressure to them, he finally coaxed her to lower her feet to the ground, but she refused to release her strong hold around his neck.

"We need to get you warmed up, Mimi."

He grabbed a towel that Mrs. Schaeffer had laid out for her, wrapped it around her, and sealed her with his arms.

Softly crying and still shivering, she held onto him as if her life depended on it.

"Mimi, we both need to get out of these wet clothes."

She remained speechless as they stood in the middle of the room, holding on to one another.

"Mimi, if you want to get warm and stop shivering, everything is gonna have to come off of you."

She spoke through her soft cries, "I know." But she didn't move.

Somehow, he took that as permission to undress her, but not before he at least took his wet shirt off. Feeling him tug at his shirt, she lifted off him just enough to let him remove his shirt and then rested her head on his chest again and secured her arms around his trim waist.

He looked down at her, still distraught, and kissed her forehead before he reached between them and lifted her dress until he could grab the hem of it. With the dress bunched in his hands, he touched the lace band on her panties. He pushed her panties down over her smooth, curvaceous hips.

She never looked at him but continued to cling to him as she shivered.

He heard her panties finally hit the floor. Seeing that she wouldn't continue to undress herself, he reached behind him and slowly pried her hands from around his neck. "Keep your arms up," he directed her as he pulled her dress over her head. He stared into her eyes as he unfastened her bra and then quickly wrapped the towel around her.

Her hands hung at her sides as he slid his hands into

them. "Are you okay?"

She said nothing.

He could tell she was still shaken up. He escorted her over to the bed and sat her down and then sat next to her. "Mimi, say something to me. Let me know what you're thinking." He braced his chin on her head and he rubbed her back as she rested in his underarm. He kicked off his shoes, still hearing water squish in them.

She found the strength to say against his chest, "Shawn, I don't know how to swim. I could've died. I felt like I was dying, but you jumped in and saved me. You risked your life to save me." She squeezed him tighter.

"But you didn't. You're fine." He reasoned her shivering was more so from her crying than her possibly still being chilled to the bone from the water. "What else is it Mimi?"

He said her nickname with such caress in his voice as if he'd been sent specifically to earth to protect her.

It rattled her. How could someone who barely knew her show more concern for her than the woman who birthed her?

Feeling more comfortable with him than she ever had before, other than their first kiss, she kept her head low against his chest and said, "Thinking I was gonna die scared me because I was thinking I would never prove to my mother how great I could actually be. Even without her love."

"Hunh?" His forehead wrinkled. "I don't follow you."

She pulled back from him and sat up straight to look him in the eyes. "My mother has been an alcoholic the majority of my life. She barely raised me. It's like she chose liquor over me. The only time she ever really spoke to me was to berate me. She'd tell me I'd never amount to anything. I'd never be good enough. Said she wished I would've never been born." Fresh tears surfaced. "My dad died when I was young, there was no one else there to love me and be there for me. I've worked as hard as I have all of my life to show her that I made something great of myself without her." Realizing how much she had cried, she used a corner of the towel draping her body to wipe her nose.

Shawn reached up and lightly traced his finger over the small eagle tattoo on her shoulder.

Her eyelids fluttered from his touch.

"Does this tattoo have anything to do with your mom?"

"Yeah," she whispered. "It was a dare from my best friend, Dana, to get it in undergrad. I don't know why, but I was bold that day in accepting the challenge. I told myself if I was going to do it, it'd have to be meaningful. I thought it'd be silly to get an image of blueprints or something specific to architecture." She chuckled and Shawn smiled at the upward curve of her beautiful mouth.

"I learned what eagles represented back in elementary. So I decided to get it as a reminder that I'm powerful and strong and able to soar and accomplish whatever I set my mind to." She lowered her head and mumbled, "Problem is, my thoughts always shift to how I can do things to somehow please my mother."

"So that's why you're hell-bent on getting this promotion? You think you need to prove something to her?"

"Yes. That and the fact that I'm well qualified for it and deserve it." She bent her neck as she stared at him. "And what about you? What's pushing you for the promotion?"

His nostrils flared and he clenched his jaws. He didn't want to lose it in front of her with thoughts of his dad, so he prepared himself to ignore answering her question. He tried to get up from the bed, but she gripped his knee as she sat up and looked him in his eyes.

"I told you my issue. You can tell me yours," she said the last of her words just above a whisper, nervous about how strong her attraction to him had become suddenly. *Or has it been there all along?*

With his head down, he took a deep breath and pinched the bridge of his nose. He looked back up into her wanting eyes and felt ready to share his story with her. "I have an older brother who was born breech. The umbilical cord was wrapped around his neck for so long before they got him out of the womb that he showed no signs of viable life. After months of observation and many tests, the doctors said he hadn't gotten enough oxygen to his brain during birth. The whole ordeal affected the way he would develop, if ever. According to them, he wasn't supposed to make it, walk, talk, learn on his own.

"But the fact that he's a doctor now with his own practice that's just received a massive grant adds to the list of reasons why my father has adored him more than he ever did me over the years. It's like I'm invisible to my dad." He sighed. "But I don't want to unload my burdens on you."

He seemed to bear the same heaviness about his dad as she did with her mother. "Shawn, it's okay. I'm listening." She tightened the towel over her breasts before she squeezed his hand, encouraging him to continue.

He stared at her, wanting to kiss her, but he could tell she expected to learn more about him. He enjoyed the intimacy between them, and it propelled him to share more of his story with her.

"He was never there for any of my accomplishments because he was too busy cheering Chad on. It made me feel like no matter what I did, it would never be good enough for him in comparison to my brother's accomplishments. But it's never stopped me from trying to get his attention, his love. No matter how frustrated I get in the process."

"I can understand that." She dropped her head and twiddled her fingers in her lap. "Seems like we both have pertinent reasons for wanting this promotion, but I don't want to talk about any more of it right now."

Feeling like his quiet time with her was coming to an end, he reluctantly shifted on the bed. "Well, I'll let you change your clothes while I go change out of these wet pants." He pointed to the set of oversized clothes Mrs. Schaeffer laid out for him. But when he looked over at her, he saw a hesitancy in her eyes. Like she wasn't ready for him to leave. "Mimi, are you sure you're okay if I leave you alone? Is there something else you want, need right now?" he asked in a low, husky voice.

She opened her mouth, but nothing came out.

The air between them was charged.

She bit her bottom lip and her long eyelashes slowly fluttered.

Shawn felt the pull between them and lowered his face mere inches from hers. Their breaths mingled together.

She found words as she stared into his eyes. "Shawn, is there something else you want?" She bit her lip in nervousness again. She knew the question sounded loaded but couldn't take it back. She didn't want to.

Being so close to her biting her lip was too much

for him. He wanted to be the one biting it. He stared in her eyes, looking to see if she wanted an honest answer, and when he saw so, he said, "Mimi, I want to taste you again."

That was it. She wanted all that he had to offer.

She leaned in, giving him permission to kiss her, and he wasted no time in covering her mouth with his succulent lips.

He prodded her mouth with his tongue until she opened her lips and their tongues mingled, which heightened his senses. He grabbed the back of her head, tilting it to explore every inch of her mouth. He reveled in finally being able to bury his hands in her gorgeous head of hair. He massaged her scalp as he fervently kissed her.

She moaned as his hand played in her hair and his tongue serenaded hers.

The sounds he elicited from her made him want her that much more. His free hand caressed her inner thigh and hiked a slow path upwards.

Every inch of her body tingled for him. She wrapped her arms around his neck, pulling him closer to her. Not wanting to miss any aspect of the kiss, she turned her body more to him.

Miriam's soft whimpers and massaging of his neck as he traveled the depths of her mouth pushed him over the edge of sanity. He laid her back on the bed as they continued kissing.

On top of her, his thigh wedged in between her ample legs as he grabbed a handful of her butt.

Shawn's strong hand firmly squeezing her made her want to be even closer to him. She spread her legs wide and wrapped them around his waist.

He pulled his face from hers and broke their kiss to look her in the eyes. *Does she want more?*

She stared at him briefly before she pulled his head back down to hers and began to dominate the kiss, alternating between licking his lips and caressing his tongue with hers. Her inhibitions had fled.

Shawn gripped her butt and began to trail fervent kisses across her collar bone.

She arched her back, which made him moan and his hand slid under her towel in search of her core. Right when he was about to slide his hand into her womanly folds, there was a knock at the door. "You two okay in there?" Mrs. Schaeffer said.

Shawn huffed loudly and dropped his head on her chest. "We'll be out in a minute."

She relaxed her legs from around him and he knew their time had passed.

He looked up at her with apprehension on his face and annoyance in his voice. "We should go, hunh?"

"Yeah, I guess." Miriam found herself grabbing at the top of the towel, making sure it was still in place.

He sighed out loud again as he rested his head on her chest one more time. He let out a deep exhale as he lifted himself off her. Secure on his feet, he held his hands out to help her up.

When she was flat on her feet, and not wanting to leave her quite yet, he pulled her close to him again, interlacing his hands on the small of her back as he stared into her inquisitive eyes. He inched his face closer to hers until he could feel her breath on his face. "You sure you want me to go?"

Her eyes shifted away from his stare and she whispered, "Yes." She bit her bottom lip and curves of frustration and confusion etched her forehead.

"Okay." He sighed as he slipped back into his shoes and grabbed the extra clothes from the bed. He reluctantly turned from her and ducked down to exit the low-ceiling room.

Once the door was closed, she put her hands up to her mouth. Even though moments had passed since his lips last touch hers, she could still feel the effects of his kiss. She patted them to see if her lips were really as swollen as they felt after the tantalizing kiss they had shared yet again.

22

Miriam walked into her guest bedroom at the Schaeffer's beach house. She closed the door behind her and laid against it. She was grateful to be past the Schaeffer's nonstop questioning as to whether or not she was okay. She appreciated their concern, but her brain was too rattled from what she experienced that night with Shawn.

From the moment he cradled her in his arms when rescuing her from the water to him pressing his forehead against hers before he finally left the bedroom on the boat, everything about him screamed he genuinely cared for her. *How is it possible for a man who barely knows me to kiss me with such tenderness and fervor at the same time? As if I'm all he wants. If Mrs. Schaeffer hadn't knocked on the door, would I have gone all the way with him?*

She questioned herself as she lifted off the door and

walked to her suitcase. She grabbed what she needed to shower. *Maybe a hot shower will calm the uneasiness in my stomach. I'm not sure if it's from almost drowning or from my time spent with Shawn tonight.*

She walked over to the bathroom door, pressed her ear against it and held her breath, listening to hear if Shawn was in the bathroom. She wasn't ready to see him again. She was still coming down from her high with him earlier. Too many thoughts and emotions were swarming her to know how she really felt about him or how she would react, how far she'd go if she got close to him again. If he kissed her again.

A slight smile crept on her face, and before she knew it, she was stroking her lips with the pads of her fingers, remembering how Shawn tasted. When a wide smile had plastered her face, she shook her head, trying to jolt herself from her reverie of what they shared.

Refocusing her attention, she realized she didn't hear anything on the other side of the door. She pulled it open, stepped in the bathroom and went over to the other door that led to Shawn's temporary room and twisted the knob. She needed to know it was locked.

When satisfied that she had some type of privacy, she stripped out of the clothes Mrs. Schaeffer had left out for her. Although they were the same size as most of the clothes she had in her closet, she realized how ridiculously large they were given her svelte frame. It took wearing someone else's clothes, the same sizes as hers, to realize that Dana had been right all along; her clothes were way too big for her. Even though she knew she wore the baggy clothes to ward off unwanted attention at work.

She quickly stilled her thoughts, fearing she heard movement in Shawn's room. After moments of silence, she turned the showerhead on, balled her hair up into a ponytail on top of her head and jumped in the shower.

She lathered up with her lavender almond-scented body wash and relished in the hot water beating on her back. The heat from it in no way matched the fire between her and Shawn earlier that evening. And just like that, thoughts of him, touching her, kissing her tumbled to the front of her mind. *What did he really mean when he said he wanted to taste me?* She bit her lip thinking of how good his mouth would feel on her core if his kisses were able to suspend her consciousness the way they did.

Tired of the pulsing ache between her legs and battling thoughts of him in her mind, she silently admitted to herself that she was attracted to him. She could agree that he wasn't self-centered like she imagined him to be for all those years.

He actually endeared her with his genuine concern for her. His comfort for her that night touched depths of her heart she didn't even know existed. *As much as I understand his motive for wanting the position, and how I'll be forever grateful to him for saving my life, I still want and deserve that promotion.* "That promotion is mine." Reminding herself of what was at stake, she realized she couldn't be involved with Shawn no matter what.

The stakes were high.

If he got the promotion, she thought she might resent him for it, and it would eventually sever any romantic efforts on their parts.

If she got the promotion, it only made sense to her that Shawn would resent her for getting the one accomplishment he felt his dad would finally be proud of. "That's it. No Shawn in my present or in my future," she said out loud and turned the shower off. *I need to get sleep and be well-rested for my presentation tomorrow.* "I got this."

She grabbed a towel from the rack and wrapped it around her body, picked up her strewn clothes from the floor and left the bathroom to finish readying herself for bed as she heard the shower turn on.

***

Maybe Miriam hadn't heard him at the door after all. He was trying not to be a creep, but he was already at the bathroom door, ready to turn the knob when it rattled without his touch. He figured it was her checking to see if it was locked.

Rather than tiptoeing across the squeaky hardwood

floors and alert her of his movements, he stood still at the door.

He waited until he heard the water running before he made his way over to the window and stared at the moon's reflection on the seemingly black waters. He needed to take a shower too, but honestly, he'd much rather take one with her than alone.

His attraction to her wasn't only sexual, but he'd be damned if he lied to himself and pretended like he didn't want to pin her against the shower wall, hold her thigh up and go as deep into her as he could. Over and over again until they both were sated.

The faint scent of whatever she was using to wash with made his manhood pulse, imagining suds bubbling over what he knew to be perky breasts. "Damn. Why did Mrs. Schaeffer interrupt us? Even if we didn't go all the way, I could've tasted what I've been wanting to," he cursed again under his breath and looked down to see what the effects of the images in his head had done to him.

He rubbed his neck. *Although I know she was busy fielding questions from the Schaeffer's on the walk back from the pier, she clearly ignored me. Does she only think I want sex from her? Naw, that can't be it. The way she opened up to me tonight and the way I opened up to her, she has to know I truly care about her.*

When he heard her bedroom door close, he grabbed his toiletries and made his way to the bathroom.

He turned the shower on and let the water subdue his face as he thought about everything. He very much still wanted the position, but after learning Miriam's motivation, he imagined her childhood and felt like his reason for the promotion paled in comparison to hers.

It's not like he never received any love growing up. His mother was always there to pick up the slack where he lacked affection from his dad. Although she clearly could never replace a father's love towards his son.

By the time he turned the showerhead off, he was firm in his desire to show Miriam the love she didn't have growing up. If that meant he would scale back his proposal to let her win, that was a chance he would take.

23

Shawn woke up, groggy. Between naughty images of Miriam surfacing, causing his manhood to stay at attention, and the gnawing prompting that he should finally settle things with his father, he barely got a full hour of sleep.

He closed his eyes many times, but multiple thoughts attacked him so that his eyes would pop open and he'd play out varying endings to the things he knew he should do.

He didn't close his curtains the night before, so he laid in bed, shielding his eyes from the sunlight beaming directly on his face.

Groaning, he rolled over and got out of bed. He went and stood in front of the glass sliding door that led to the balcony off his room, braced his hands on his lower back then stretched backward and forward, allowing his hands to hang to the ground.

When he stood up straight, he knew the new day meant he had business to take care of. He would've loved to dress and head down to breakfast in hopes that Miriam would be there eating too. He wanted to gauge her mood, see how she would be around him before they went to the studio, but there was an important matter he had to settle.

He would've called him the moment he made the decision to clear the air with him, but a 2:30am conversation didn't seem so favorable at the time.

He went in and grabbed his phone from the charger, sat in the bedside, plush high back chair and dialed his father's number.

Vincent Lafayette had always been an early riser, so it was no surprise to him when his father answered the phone sounding chipper.

"Good morning, Dad. How are you?"

"Good morning, son. I'm great. How are you?"

"Good. You got a second to talk?"

"Sure, your brother won't be over for another hour and then we're gonna start the grill up. Come over and join us later on."

Shawn rubbed his face trying to quell his brooding anger. Not only had his father not invited him in on the bonding time most men have grilling together, his father diminished him to coming over later, after the men spent time together cooking. Where was his pre-notice for the day's festivities?

But he couldn't let his anger for what he felt was his dad's neglect of him go on any longer. He took a deep breath, stood up, and began to pace the floor.

"Shawn, are you still there?"

"Yes, sir."

"Is everything okay?"

He paused before sighing and said, "No, Dad. It's not. It's never been okay."

"What hasn't been okay?" Vincent stepped away from his tool bench in his garage and walked to stand in the doorway overlooking his expansive and lush backyard.

"I know it'd be better if we had this conversation face to face, but I fear if I wait any longer, I'll just keep sweeping it under the rug."

"Well, why don't you come over and we can talk about it."

"I can't, Dad. I'm out of town for work."

"Okay, but tell me what it is, son. You're starting to make me nervous."

Shawn stopped pacing the floor. His emotions had lodged in his throat and he knew he couldn't talk just yet. He needed to compose himself. In his remembrance, he'd never heard such concern in his father's voice for him.

"Shawn, you still there, son? Whatever it is, you can tell me. I won't judge you. You should know that." Vincent stepped out into his backyard.

Shawn cleared his throat and decided to just spit out what he had to say. "Why don't you love me the way you love Chad?"

Vincent stopped kicking back into place the strewn pebbles from the perimeter of a walkway that went from the garage out to a firepit surrounded by seats.

He looked at the phone as if it were a foreign object foreign and then put it back up to his ear. "Did you just ask why I don't love you as much as I love Chad?"

"Yes, sir."

"Why would you even ask me a question like that, Shawn? Where would you get such an absurd idea from?" Vincent braced his free hand on his waist as his forehead scrunched. "I thought I did a good job over the years showing you boys just how much I love you each."

"You did a great job showing Chad and me just how much you loved him. I never saw your love for me," Shawn snipped.

"Shawn, what do you mean you never saw my love for you? I wasn't a good father to you?" Vincent ambled over to the cooler he had situated next to the grill and sat on it. Shawn's statement unsettled him, and he needed to bear his footing. "Shawn, why don't you think I love you?"

Shawn choked on his tears of frustration. "You were never there to celebrate me at my big stuff. You chose going to both Chad's championship game and college graduation over mine. You always went to cheer him on if we had something on the same day.

"Whenever Chad accomplishes something, he gets parties, and these long drawn out speeches. Your fanfare for him is large, but whenever I do something, I just get a pat on the back from you, if that."

Vincent opened his mouth to speak, but Shawn kept talking, so he let him.

"Seems like every time I come to you with some good news, Chad always has an announcement, another accomplishment to overshadow my success and you bask in his success rather than mine or both of ours equally. I want to be celebrated too. I want to know that you're proud of me."

"I am, son."

"But you don't show it. Why can't you and I be close like you and Chad?" Shawn kicked at his shoes in front of him.

"I thought we were close. I always told you boys that you could come and talk to me about anything."

"Yeah, dad, but it's different with you and me versus you and Chad. Perfect example, you told me I could come over later, but Chad is probably there by now ready to fire up the grill with you. You two agreed on meeting this morning. You'll bond over God knows what, but I didn't even get an invite to come over to the house today."

"But you don't ever need an invite to come home,

ever, Shawn."

"You just don't get it, dad." Shawn huffed. "Who thought up the grill fest this morning?"

There was silence on the other end of Shawn's phone.

"Right. You took the time out to invite Chad over but didn't bother to call me. Another example as to why I feel the way I do. You never ask me questions about me. I bet you don't even know I'm up for promotion to be senior executive architect."

Vincent's eyes widened. "You are?"

"Yes. That's what I'm here in South Carolina for. I present later, but not until I take another shot at winning over the heart of the woman I love." Shawn paused, realizing what he'd said out loud to his dad. He hadn't even admitted that truth to himself.

"What? You're in a serious relationship?" Vincent stood to his feet and pressed the phone closer to his ear.

"No—"

"You're in love with a woman, but not in a relationship with her?" Vincent walked the path toward the firepit. "I'm not following you."

"One issue at a time, dad. I've been grinding all my life trying to win your approval. I never pursued her for pretty much the past decade and put aside my sincere interest in her because I was too focused on trying to get this promotion to get you to notice me. Get you to see that you had another son worth paying attention to." He let out a deep sigh.

"Shawn, you know what the deal was with your brother when he was born. It was a miracle that he made it, that he's accomplished all that he has. I just want him to know that he can continue to do whatever he puts his mind to."

"Yeah, Dad, you were there for him. You showed him that you cared for him. That you believed in him, but you never did any of that stuff for me."

"Shawn, I was there for you."

"No, Dad, you were there for Chad."

"You sent mom to all of my games. You went to Chad's graduation instead of mine. You went to his championship games instead of mine.

"I know you didn't schedule all of our major events to be on the same day, but you could have alternated your attendance between us. It would have been nice to look up in the stands and see my father cheering me on. Showing me that he was proud of me."

Vincent took a deep breath as he thought back over the years and realized that he had missed all of Shawn's major milestones in sports and academics. A tear trickled down his face. He never wanted his sons to think that he didn't love them. "Shawn, if I would've known that you felt this way all along, I would've tried to do things differently and a lot sooner. Why didn't you ever tell me?"

"Because Dad, why should a son have to teach and

show their father how to love them?"

Vincent remained silent.

"Besides, I knew you knew how to love because you showed Chad, you just never showed me." Shawn blew out an exasperated breath. "I know that it's time, way past time to get over it and move on to new things I want in my life. Whether I get this promotion or not, I'm going to be happy. Whether you cheer me on or not, I'm going to be happy. I just hope that it can be with the woman that I love."

Vincent slowly rubbed a hand over his face. "Well, son, I'm glad that you told me this now. I'll try my best from now on to do better to show you just how much I love you and how proud I am of you."

Vincent was still shaken from what Shawn had shared with him. The moment called for a cigar to relax his mind. He always thought he was fair with both his sons, but Shawn had just proven otherwise. He had to take Shawn at his word. He was readying himself to get off the phone when Shawn's last statement rang oddly in his head. "And what do you mean you just hope that you get this promotion? Shawn, you're great. You're a genius. I know that you'll get the promotion."

"Thanks, Dad, but I'm not so sure about getting the promotion now. I think there's someone more deserving of it than I am. I'd rather have her love than the promotion."

"Well, son, I hope I get to meet this woman sooner

than later. And again, I'm sorry for making you feel that I didn't love you over the years but just know that I love you from the bottom of my heart. Always have. Always will."

"Thanks, Dad. I love you too. We'll catch up when I get back, but Artemis is on the other line."

"Okay. Tell him I said hi and to behave himself." Vincent chuckled.

Shawn smirked. "I'll tell him, dad, but you know how he is. I think it'll be hard for him."

They both laughed before Shawn switched over to the other line. "Artemis, what's up bro?"

"Just checking on you. Have you made your move with her yet? Had another kiss with her?"

"Man, I'm not gonna kiss and tell."

"You did before, so I don't know what the difference is with this time."

"Don't worry about that?"

"Well, stop tellin' me your business if you don't want me in it. Shoot, you're the one who texted me and told me that you were going on the show again with her. What kind of fool tells their business but don't want nobody in it? I'll tell you what kind, the crazy kind."

Artemis stopped brushing the waves in his head. He leaned over his bathroom counter to get a closer look in the mirror at a blackhead on his face. "Wondering about you has my face breaking out. I'mma have to stop by my barber for a facial first thing in the morning, but tonight, I'mma party." He swayed to the music in his head.

Shawn shook his head. "You called to talk about me or you?"

Artemis pulled his phone away from his ear and stared at it with his face marred as if an alien were on the other line. "Shawn, you buggin' out, boy. You texted me about going to the show and trying to get her." He pulled the phone back away from his face, stared at it and said, "What is wrong with this fool?"

"I heard you." Shawn laughed, knowing with how faint Artemis's voice was, he may not have wanted him to hear what he said.

Artemis put the phone back up to his ear. "Good. I ain't scared of you, chump."

They both laughed.

"Nah, for real ship, did you go to the show yet?"

Shawn breathed a deep sigh. "Not yet. I just hope that the odds work in my favor when we do."

"They will. You're a great guy. Any woman would be lucky to have you."

"What is this, you getting all sentimental on me?" Shawn said.

"Naw, I'm just saying man, you have to be. You're my line brother. Weren't no chumps allowed on S.S.D.O.W.N. And everybody can't be a player like me. Some dudes got to be the ones willing to settle down with these ladies out here. May not be for me, but you go for it."

Shawn sucked his teeth. "Man, every player has thought that until that one woman came along and changed their mind. You saying that now, but sooner than later, when she comes along, you'll be tapping some different keys on that piano of your understanding."

"Man, I guess big brother let a loose cannon in the fraternity after all because you don't have any sense. Shawn, I ain't met the one I would commit to. Starting to think I won't. Next topic. Ready for the presentation? I know you got that promotion in the bag."

"I'm not so sure about that."

"Why you doubting yourself now, fool?" Artemis's voice pitched higher.

"Because man, although I won't kiss and tell, I will say that we've gotten closer this weekend and I think that she's more deserving of it than I am." Shawn rubbed his head.

"So what are you saying, you gon' throw it so that you give it to her?"

"I don't know, man, we'll see. I'll let you know when I get back. Gotta go."

"Sh-Shawn—"

Shawn hung up the phone despite Artemis, trying to get his attention.

24

Miriam walked into the blank space with tall ceilings trying to figure out how it played a part in the design for the hotel. But she decided not to let that be her concern. If Mr. Schaeffer thought that she and Shawn needed to see it before their presentation, then she needed to be there.

"Hello," a man with a headset on said to Miriam as he walked past her.

"Hello." She nodded her head with one eyebrow raised.

Shawn buried his smile.

Soon a woman with a long flowing dress walked up to Miriam and extended her hand to shake it. "So glad you can make it here today. Follow me this way you all." She smiled and turned to lead the way.

Not wanting to talk to him or make eye contact after

what they shared the night before, but needing to make sense of where they were, Miriam looked back briefly at him as they followed behind the woman. "Do you know why we're here? What does this place have to do with the hotel?"

Shawn squashed the laughter brewing in him and said, "I'm not sure. Let's just follow the lady and see what's what."

Not satisfied with his answer and no longer able to look at him without her stomach performing a gold medal-worthy routine on a gymnastics floor, Miriam turned back to face the direction they were walking in. The sensations he caused her were well past those of fluttering butterflies.

They made it through a heavy black door at the end of the hallway and Miriam began to see familiar faces, many of which had headsets on. There were rolling tripods with cameras centered on them. But the dead giveaway as to why she was there was when she spotted the executive producer, Mark, of the show, "The Kissing Game", making his way towards her.

He was the one that introduced her to Shawn's lips, so she knew that her being there had nothing to do with the hotel or her presentation but everything to do with Shawn and their first kiss.

Miriam bore a pinched expression as her jaws clenched. She turned her narrowed eyes on Shawn and pointed at him. "You had something to do with this, didn't you?"

Shawn shrugged his shoulders and lifted his hands in the air. "I, I, I—" Shawn was ready to deny his part in her being there, but Miriam cut him off.

"Save it. You had to have a part in getting me here. Mr. Schaeffer didn't know, only you and I knew about the show, the kiss..." Her words trailed off as her imagination managed to give way to just how incredible Shawn's lips, his body felt against hers. She had never experienced anything as endearing, magical as she had when she kissed him. She never thought she would again, but the kiss they shared the night before proved her wrong. There was a sincerity, a maturity to his craft of kissing, a connection with him that had her willing to throw away her reservations about him, about them, until Mrs. Schaeffer knocked on the door and brought her back to her senses.

Standing as close to him as she was, slowly alternating between looking into his eyes and staring at his lips, threatened to undo her resolve again and throw herself into his arms, but Mark clearing his voice and appearing next to her stilled her imaginings.

"Miriam, it doesn't matter who got you here. What matters is that you're here and we're so excited about it."

She looked to the left of her. "Sorry to put the kibosh on your joy, but I won't be staying for whatever it is you want me here for." She was too close to giving her presentation to worry about anything other than landing the promotion. She needed to get out of there, and soon.

She moved over and took swift steps past Shawn, hoping he would sense her resurgence of anger for getting her there under false pretenses, but he gently grabbed her wrist to keep her from fleeing. His touch quieted her anger. She took a deep breath, trying to calm the sensations he caused her body.

Mark ran around in front of Miriam. "Please don't run out again like you did the last time."

Everyone in the studio paused.

"I can't do this right now." Miriam briefly closed her eyes and inhaled a slow, calming breath. With his fingertips, Shawn was tracing feather-like circles on the inside of her wrist. Her body enjoyed the act.

"Yes, you can. You should. I would really love to film an interview of you and Shawn, post kiss." Mark's eyebrows raised as he watched Miriam's head slightly roll back with her eyes closed. Seizing the time he had her in front of him, he continued talking, "You just don't know that out of all the footage that we watched from ten cities since we started filming this season, you all's kiss was the best.

"It's clear that you all have true passion. There's something special between you two and that kiss exposed it."

Shawn caressing her wrist and Mark's description

of the kiss still had Miriam in a euphoric trance to which she was trying to pull herself from. Her eyelids fluttered before she finally fixed her stare on Mark.

"We're going to air the kiss, but we're certain that our viewers are going to want to know exactly what happened with you all after that kiss. Shoot, I want to know. I'm excited and I know everyone else in the studio is eager to find out what's going on between you two." Mark looked down. "I mean with the way his touch is affecting you, I can only imagine how you two are, could be with no one around."

Miriam blushed but snatched her arm from Shawn's grasp. He had too much of an effect on her. She always kept her composure, no matter what the situation was, but since their first kiss, she couldn't say that anymore where Shawn was concerned.

Mark continued his pleas. "Miriam, the kiss you two shared embodies what we're trying to accomplish with the show. To show the world that two people can just know that they are meant for each other without even seeing each other. Something as simple, yet as powerful as a single kiss can bond two people together."

Miriam could sense and smell that Shawn had come closer to her. She closed her eyes and took a deep breath. They didn't understand that the bond Mark spoke of was something that she had been toying with ever since that kiss. Last night made it even more apparent to her just how connected she really was to

Shawn.

She couldn't trust herself.

She felt that any more time spent with him, near him, smelling the scent of his cologne would send her right into his arms and her lips plastered over his. But she had been saved from crossing a line the night before.

Although she wanted him badly, maybe it was a sign that she shouldn't get caught up with him.

Shawn stepped even closer to her and held on to her waist as he leaned down to whisper in her ear. "Mimi, let's just give the interview a try. Please?"

The heat of his breath tickled her ear, moistened her center, and elevated her desire for him. She turned and looked up at him. Although she had stared into his eyes before, she wasn't prepared to look into them. They were gorgeous. They were inviting. They were sincere. They made it hard for her to deny his pleas, no matter how much that nagging inner voice of hers wanted to. "Okay," she said, barely audible.

He smiled a lazy, sexy smile as he squeezed her waist, then stepped aside to allow her to walk in front of him.

Mark clapped his hands rapidly and squealed with delight before commanding everyone on set to take their places.

The same guy who mic'd Miriam up for her first kiss with Shawn walked up and said, "Hey sweetie, so glad to see you back here. I wonder if I'll get a chance to see another one of those kisses between you two. It's been my template for kisses ever since."

Miriam gave him a half-smile. Had the kiss really impacted others even as half as much as it had her?

Still unsure of how to feel about her and Shawn, she desperately wanted to get through the interview and get on to her presentation and nail it because every time she thought about Shawn or looked at him, she forgot all about it as if it weren't the most important thing to her.

She was escorted to sit on a loveseat next to Shawn.

"We're ready for some more magic." Mark took his place behind a camera.

Fake applause could be heard in the studio as the host of the show, Dee Phillips, smiled and stared into camera one. "Hello everyone and welcome back to the follow-up show of 'The Kissing Game', featuring the couple of kissers we all have come to love, Miriam Caldwell and Shawn Lafayette." She smiled at them.

There was another round of engineered applause echoing throughout the studio.

"Before we get caught up on your post first kiss antics, let's look at that first kiss as a quick reminder of what brought you all here."

Camera one switched from Dee and to a big screen showing a replay of the kiss between Miriam and Shawn.

Miriam shifted in her seat. Her breathing labored as she stared at the screen, watching Shawn walk in the room before he made it over to her and they eventually got lost in the kiss.

It was one thing to experience the kiss firsthand with him, but to see it on the high definition big screen caused her to see just how people could gather how passionate the kiss was and how attracted to each other they had been.

Shawn held a smile on his face the entire time the kiss played. He was there. He knew exactly how it felt to hold her in his arms and explore every crevice of her mouth. He admitted that it looked as good on camera as it felt when he held her.

"Okay, folks. Now that we have you all caught up, let's get down to what you really want to know, how the lovely couple is doing since that smoking hot kiss." She turned and looked at Miriam first. "Miriam, how has it been for you two?"

Dazed and still unsure of herself or her feelings for Shawn, Miriam said nothing.

Too many seconds of silence on set forced Dee to turn her attention to Shawn. "So, Shawn, how has it been for the two of you?"

Shawn cleared his throat and adjusted in his seat as he straightened his slacks. "Well, Dee, it's been interesting. You see—"

Miriam shot him a questioning look.

He gathered it meant not to expose her and place all the blame at her feet.

Although technically she was the only reason they weren't together, he figured outing her to the world wouldn't get him any closer to winning her over.

He said nothing else.

Dee looked at Mark, moving his hand in a circular motion, encouraging her to keep going. She turned back to the main camera and said, "We'll be right back after we get these parched lovebirds some water."

"Cut," Mark yelled. "Shawn, I thought you agreed to come on and discuss you all," Mark said through a fake smile as he scurried up to them.

"I did, and I'm here, but I can't make her talk," Shawn said. "And I don't want to say anything that will make her uncomfortable." He stared at her.

Mark turned his attention to Miriam. "Won't you please do the interview for us? We'll pay you. What's your price? Roderick, get legal and accounting on the phone now," he screamed, even though his personal assistant, Roderick, was right next to him.

"That won't be necessary. My privacy is not for hire."

"But you and Shawn are just what this show needs, what America needs to see that true love at first kiss does exist," he said with his hands in front of her in a praying motion.

Miriam looked over at Shawn for a moment to see if he could help her get out of the bind with the producer, but her thoughts dissipated into nothingness when she locked eyes with him. In them, was no question of how he felt about her. He believed in love at first kiss.

She opened and closed her dry mouth, struggling to say anything. Anything that would get Mark to see things her way.

She dug deep in herself, pulled her focus from Shawn and faced Mark again.

Miriam rattled off the reasons why they couldn't be together. "Why don't you all understand that Shawn and I won't work?"

"Miriam, but how do you know if you don't give it a try?" Mark asked.

"I just know that it won't work. What work relationship do you know of that has lasted the test of time? For heaven's sake, we're up for the same position. What if he gets it and we're together? I can hear people in the office talking now. Saying stuff like, 'Oh she's sleeping with the boss'."

Shawn smiled at the mention of them sleeping together. He'd love for that to happen sooner than later, but Miriam's rant brought his thoughts back to the present.

"I can hear them saying it now, 'Oh, she must get special privileges'. Or what if I get it and we're together? I won't be taken seriously as a woman, a black woman, in the workplace, sleeping with one of my employees. I can't do this..." She kept talking as if she were trying to convince herself more so than them why they wouldn't work out.

Shawn silenced her with a loud huff. "Mimi, it's not my damn fault that you're so lovable. I didn't make your cute nose. I don't force you to do that sexy thing of pushing your glasses up the bridge of your nose. I didn't create those kissable lips of yours, but I do enjoy them." He winked at her.

She was red and flustered with excitement and embarrassment.

He continued with his admiration of her. "I didn't force you to consume my thoughts all of these years."

Her forehead furrowed.

He noticed her look of confusion. "Yes, Miriam, I've always been attracted to you. Wanted to know more about you. Date you. But just like you focused at work all these years, you know why I did the same.

"When we kissed the first time, although I knew it had to be something special about that kisser, I was secretly hoping it was you." He reached over and grabbed her hand and stroked the back of it with his thumb as he stared into her eyes. "I'm not saying that I know everything there is to know about you, but I do know that I want you. Promotion or not."

She said nothing.

It looked as if she held her breath as she bit her bottom lip, staring at him with a mixture of nervousness and want. He leaned in to kiss her and once again, the attraction between them pulled her to him and she was eager to give in to her desire to kiss him again.

She tilted her head to the side, ready for a full-on kiss, but she looked past him and at the big clock on the wall. It showed they had thirty minutes before the agenda scheduled them to be in Mr. Schaeffer's office for their presentations.

She stalled just short of his lips and said, "I can't do this, Shawn." She stood to rush off, but Shawn's firm, yet gentle grip on her hand kept her from moving as he stood up and towered her.

He lifted her chin, forcing her to finally look at him again. "Yes, you can, Mimi. Yes, we can. We can make this work. There's too much of a pull between us for it not to work."

She searched his eyes. They seared her understanding of just how much he wanted her, but knowing where she was headed, she was willing to sacrifice a future with him if it finally meant showing her mother just how special she really was. She spoke barely above a whisper, "I can't, Shawn. I have to go."

She felt her eyes water as she rushed off. She couldn't chance being in the car with him back to the beach house and have him convince her to give them a chance. Any more moments spent with him, staring into his eyes, and she'd yield to his sincerity for her, her desire to be with him.

She made it outside of the studio and hailed a cab to take her back to the Schaeffer's. The moment her back hit the seat, tears shimmied down her face.

***

"Hello. I need you to calm me down. Tell me a joke. Say something to help me focus before I go into this presentation," Miriam said into her phone as she wiped tears from her face.

"What? What's going on with you?" Dana sat up on the couch in Miriam's living room and turned the TV to mute.

"You will not believe that Shawn conspired with the producer of 'The Kissing Game' to interview me about us as if we've been an item all of this time. The producer just kept talking about the chemistry between us and he showed the kiss again." She paused and traveled down memory lane to their magnetic kisses.

"Miriam? Miriam are you still there?"

"Yes." She blinked, snapping back to the present.

"I was talking to you and you didn't say anything."

"Oh, I'm sorry. I got lost in thought for a second."

"Yeah, you were thinking about that kiss again."

"No, I'm just so frustrated. I should just be focusing on presenting, but instead, I now have to calm down from that ambush. Ugh. He infuriates me."

"Why, because you want him? You're just scared."

"I'm not scared."

"Yes, you are, Miriam."

Miriam was tired of Shawn being the subject of discussion. "Anyway, thanks for making me wear more fitted clothes. I think that I'm going to have to go shopping and update my wardrobe when I get back."

Dana's brow lifted. "Yes, you do. What happened to give you that change of heart?"

"Because, wearing fitted clothes this weekend didn't make me antsy. I just see things differently now. Before, I wanted to solely be judged for my design and engineering talents and not my small waist versus my full bosom, or my curvy and full hips, and especially not this bubble butt of mine. But now, I don't think wearing more form-fitting clothes will bring the wrong attention to me after all. I'll go shopping Monday after work. I'm sure you'll love to tag along for that excursion and pretend to be my stylist."

"You know I will and yes, I agree to all you said, but you changed the subject from the bigger issue. Are you going to give Shawn a chance?"

The car slowly rolled up to the beach house. Miriam needed to get in the house and spruce up for her presentation. "No, Dana. I don't have time to focus on that, him, right now. I'll call you back after all this is over or I'll see you when I get back to the house. Bye."

"Miriam, wait. Don't hang up."

Miriam ended the call, paid the cab driver, and got out of the car.

She walked up to the beach house taking deep

breaths, trying to calm herself and clear her mind for her presentation.

25

Miriam slowed her steps and took deep breaths as she followed behind Rosa to Mr. Schaeffer's study. She heard laughter and could tell that Mr. Pierce had come and joined the group.

Shawn's deep and rich laugh made her stop in her tracks. *What has him so happy in spite of knowing he'll soon learn his fate for the promotion? Has it already been given to him and they are merely laughing at the idea of a woman actually thinking that she can help lead the firm as an S.E.A.?*

Rosa looked back at her with a calming smile.

Miriam nodded her head and Rosa opened the door to the study.

By the time Miriam made it across the threshold, all of the gentlemen were standing.

She planned to carry on as if her nerve endings weren't tap dancing on every viable organ of hers.

Architecture and design were her passions, and her

gifts. She would govern herself in the meeting as she would in any other one she had over the years.

She smiled at everyone but Shawn. She refused to look in his direction. By then, she was no fool to how her body responded to him. When she allowed her mind to roam free with thoughts of them together, the explicit thoughts conjured up should've been illegal. There was no room to frolic in her mind at the time.

"Mr. Schaeffer, Mr. Pierce." She switched her briefcase over to her left hand and shook each of the gentlemen's hands.

Shawn cleared his throat with a smirk on his face and waited for her to acknowledge him. When she didn't, the other two men looked at each other and laughed before Shawn said, "Hello again to you too, Miriam."

Not wanting to be totally rude in front of the men who held the next phase of her future in their hands, she said, between tight lips and a fake smile, "Shawn."

Although she was still pissed at him for being in cahoots with the producer of the show to corner her about her feelings for him, it was becoming harder to resist him. She wondered if he knew just how much of an effect his smell, his essence had on her. It literally made the hairs on her arms stand up.

She still wasn't ready to admit it out loud, but she knew that only a man with a genuine interest in a woman would do the things Shawn had done to get her attention.

I mean, after all, the man did risk his life to save mine. For that he deserves my undying love, right?

"Miriam? Miriam? You ready to get this started?"

"Hunh?" Miriam tore her eyes away from Shawn's intense stare. She didn't even know that she had locked eyes with him. *See, this is why we won't work. How in the heck would I ever be able to focus on anything else other than him at work? In life? If only he didn't work at the firm, I just might give him a chance. Shoot, I would give myself a chance with him.* Miriam cleared her throat, trying to dismiss her thoughts of Shawn.

"Yes, I was saying that we're ready for the both of your final pitches as to why your designs and engineering ideas should be chosen for the hotel chain. We looked them over while you all were away this morning and I have to say, they both were extremely impressive, making our decision a tough one. But either way, the hotel will come out wonderfully and Mr. Pierce will be fine having either of you directly under him," Mr. Schaeffer said.

"We've decided to let you go first Miriam," Mr. Pierce said, resting his chin on his clasped hands. He was ready to focus on her presentation.

"Wait," Shawn said.

Miriam's head cocked toward him.

Shawn wouldn't allow her to present, knowing he had something very important to say. He toyed with his decision the night before but was sure of it when he talked with his father earlier that morning. "If you'll allow me to speak, Mimi, Miriam? I won't be long."

The calm in his voice and the tenderness in his eyes towards her jumbled up her feelings. On the one hand, she despised the fact that he interrupted her, but the way in which he said her name and stared at her, her insides welcomed his interruption.

She nodded her head with pursed lips.

"Mr. Pierce, Mr. Schaeffer, I appreciate being a candidate for the promotion, and you sir," he extended his hand to Mr. Schaeffer, "for favoring my plans for your hotel chain during the site tour, but after this weekend, I don't desire the promotion as I did before. There's something else I want more." He looked over at Miriam.

She began to fidget with the collar of her shirt.

He looked back to the men on the other side of the table. "During this weekend, I learned my reasons pale in comparison to why she wants and deserves this promotion. I'd rather it be given to her. If you all don't mind, I'll just go up to my room and let her solely present to you all."

Miriam stood slack-jawed with her eyes wide, unable to form sentences.

Shawn reached across the table and shook both men's hands before he grabbed his briefcase and headed towards the door.

Smelling the scent of his cologne waning, Miriam

realized he was almost out of the room and needed to say something, stand her ground. She ran and jumped in front of him, halting his steps.

"Now you wait a minute." She poked him in his chest as she looked up at him. "I don't want this promotion because *you* give it to me. I want this promotion because I deserve it. Stay here and let them judge whose idea is the best."

"Stay here in this room and present or stay here with you?" He stroked the side of her face.

Miriam closed her eyes briefly and leaned into his hand. Any nearness to him endeared her, but the ginger way he spoke as he looked at her dumbfounded her. She took a deep breath and opened her eyes. It only made her stare into his wanting eyes.

"Shawn…" Her voice was barely above a whisper. "I want you, but we just can't be."

A smile stretched across his face. "You said you want me?"

Her forehead wrinkled and she began to stutter, "No, I didn't."

"Yes, you did."

"No, I didn't." She took two steps back, trying to put distance between them, but he took two steps toward her.

"Mimi, you did say it."

She stepped back from him and said, "And would you stop calling me Mimi. It's annoying." She looked to say anything to deflect the heated moment between them.

He smirked as he walked up to her again and stared down into her eyes. "No, it's not. I think you secretly love it when I call you that."

She rolled her eyes, but the act only aided in widening his smile. "Admit to yourself what you haven't since our first kiss. You want me. You want us."

She bit her lip, staring at the way he slowly mouthed the end of his statement. His penetrating eyes had her ready to melt.

"I can't. I can't let you give me the position. I can't be your boss and date you. And I wouldn't know how to behave around you working under you."

"Under me?" His eyes grew darker.

She stepped back from him, needing clear air to breathe. Their breaths mingling together was making her forget why they couldn't be together.

"Stop being stubborn and let me love you the way I want to."

Miriam's eyes bucked in shock at his admission, but she couldn't muster the nerve to verbally respond.

"Are you two done yet?" Mr. Pierce cleared his throat and stood.

Mr. Schaeffer chuckled. "We were going to let you each finish your presentations before we shared what we came up with, but with the way you're fighting your feelings for him, Miriam, we'd be here all day."

Miriam craned her neck around Shawn to look at the bulging belly duo on the other side of the desk.

She gave one last dazed look at Shawn before she took pained steps towards Mr. Schaeffer and Mr. Pierce. She didn't know what to make of her fate at the time. *Did Shawn mess things up for me? Or had I done that all by myself?*

Miriam covered her face in shame. She took a deep breath and looked back at the men. "Mr. Schaeffer, Mr. Pierce, please forgive me for my lack of professionalism where Shawn and I are concerned. This is not the way I normally behave. And I can assure you both I will never carry on like this again." Though highly embarrassed, she still kept her head high and made eye contact with them.

"Please, both of you have a seat." Mr. Schaeffer propped his hand out towards the chairs neither of them had sat in yet.

"If it's okay with you, I'd rather remain standing and learn my fate," Miriam said.

Shawn walked up and stood side by side with her, making sure his arm touched hers. He just knew his presence had the same effect on her as hers did on him. Why else would she behave the way she did around him? Squeamish, shortness of breath and the way she innocently bit her lip at times staring at him.

Miriam wanted to move over but knowing she had already made an improper scene in front of them, she clenched her teeth and straightened her back.

Mr. Schaeffer looked Miriam square on and said, "Well, as I said, I looked over the proposals while you all were at the studio." He smiled, knowing why they went there but could tell from Miriam's animosity toward Shawn that the plan didn't work out so well. "One particular proposal confirmed the decision I had already made."

Her shoulders slumped.

"Miriam, don't be so hasty in your assumptions. Mr. Pierce told me that was one of the things he admired most about you is your ability to be neutral when conducting business with clients. Said you were always level-headed, but I didn't witness that this weekend." He laughed.

Keeping a straight face, she screamed at herself on the inside for losing her cool when it counted the most.

Mr. Schaeffer continued, "My dear, you have been, and forgive me for saying this, but you've been a wreck when you're around Shawn."

She opened her mouth to try and explain herself, but he lifted his hand and smiled. "No need to explain. And I'm sorry if I'm overstepping my boundaries getting in you all's business, but my dear, stop running from your feelings. Shawn made me privy to what's going on between you two and why you say you two can't be together, but I say that's poppycock."

Miriam's eyes widened in shock. Everyone's

responses had been surprising her since the meeting began.

Mr. Schaeffer laughed again. "I see Shawn and the discussion of him is what riles you. Where do you think I met Mrs. Schaeffer?"

"At a tennis court?" She shrugged her shoulders.

"I could see how you would assume that, but she was once my secretary. She too was trying to be proper and not cross the lines by entering into a work relationship, but I pursued her until she had no choice but to accept the love that I was offering her. Now I know your motivation for resisting him may vary from why she resisted me, but Miriam, work romances can work and thrive. We've been married for thirty-eight years and counting. If I had to do it all over again, I would. Pursuing and loving her was the best decision I ever made."

Mr. Pierce fake coughed, trying to get Mr. Schaeffer's attention.

Mr. Schaeffer laughed. "Mr. Pierce here is protective of you and can tell that maybe you're flustered, a little embarrassed by me being in your business so much, but how could I not be when Shawn enlisted my help."

Miriam shot Shawn a stare, but this time it wasn't one where she wanted to wring his neck. Time after time again that weekend, his actions showed just how much he wanted something with her, how much he seemed to care about her.

"Plus, the old guy made me privy to the attraction between you two. In fact, he's the one who came up with the idea of getting you two here this weekend."

Miriam gasped.

Mr. Pierce smirked. "Sorry, Miriam. It's true. After that first time, I had you two in my office to announce that you both were up for the promotion, I knew there could be something special between you two and I could clearly see you planned to fight it."

"So, did you send Shawn to the show?" she asked.

Mr. Pierce's eyebrows furrowed. "Show? What show?"

Shawn leaned into Miriam, lowered his head and whispered. "He doesn't know about the show, and unless you want to share our first kiss, the one you seem hell-bent on ignoring, you may not want to continue to question him about it." Shawn stood back up and draped his clasped hands in front of him.

Miriam opened her mouth to tell him she didn't ever want to take that kiss back, couldn't forget it if she tried, but Mr. Pierce questioned her again.

"Miriam, what show?"

She just stared at him. Still in shock at all that had been said since she entered the office.

Mr. Schaeffer cleared his throat. "Seems we've lost track of the purpose of this meeting. Miriam, you are undoubtedly the one I want to spearhead the design and engineering of my hotel franchise."

She smiled as she clapped her hands together, almost leaping off the floor, but a pesky thought occurred to her. "Mr. Schaeffer, you sure you didn't make this decision just because Shawn conceded?"

Her forehead wrinkled.

Mr. Schaeffer laughed. "Didn't I say I had my person picked out this morning? Long before Shawn came in here with his heroic antics."

Miriam's smile returned with a vengeance. Her eyes gleamed.

Looking at how happy she was, Shawn knew he had made the right decision to concede but was even more happy that she had won it on her own merit. Something that he knew she would value more than anything else. Finally doing the one thing she felt would prove to her mother what she thought she needed to, even though he felt she had nothing to prove to the woman.

He turned to her and extended his hand to her for a handshake. She accepted it.

"Congratulations, Miriam. You are more than deserving of the position. I really am happy for you." His hand tingled gripping hers. He could tell she felt that kismet vibe between them too with how her eyes darted back and forth between their hands and his eyes.

He continued to hold her hand, wanting to savor the moment as long as he could. Who knew if he'd ever be that close to her again? With her essentially being his boss now, she had asserted the idea that it would be preposterous to date him.

He turned to Mr. Schaeffer and Mr. Pierce and said, "Thank you, gentlemen, for allowing me the opportunity to vie for the position and share my ideas with you all, but I'll leave you two with your new senior executive architect." He turned to walk away, but Miriam's firm grip on his hand and Mr. Schaeffer's voice kept him cemented where he was.

"While Miriam's designs lined up more with my vision for my hotels and made her the winner for the S.E.A. at the firm, Shawn, your design mind is just as sharp as hers. The minute we were done with the tour, I phoned Pierce here and told him I wanted you to be the lead architect and designer for my event venues I want to open up across the country. With Miriam designing my hotels and you designing my theaters and convention centers, I know your combined efforts will garner me millions more."

Shawn kept his glee at bay with a mere tight-lipped smile.

"It also means millions more for Pierce Industries, Shawn. I know we started this out with there only being one senior executive architect position available, but after reviewing both of you all's aggressive proposals, it only makes sense to have you both as S.E.A.s. I trust that you both, individually and collectively, will help to not only keep Pierce Industries thriving in this competitive market but solidify our standing as one of the country's top architecture firms."

Miriam's joy bubbled over as she continued to hold on to Shawn's hand. She was also happy that Shawn had gotten a promotion as well.

Before the weekend began, she didn't have anyone else to rely on other than Dana, but Shawn had proven otherwise.

He had his own reasons for wanting the promotion, but he'd put his need to prove something to his dad aside to let her prove her worth to her mother. The only thing ever done for her to top that was when he jumped in that water, ignoring his own safety, and risked his life to save her. It all showed her that she could trust him with her life. She could trust him with her heart.

Shawn attempted to free his hand from Miriam's grasp so he could shake the other men's hands in the room, but Miriam squeezed it harder and drew his full attention to her. "Shawn," she said softly, gazing into his eyes.

"Mimi." His voice was breathy, barely above a whisper.

Knowing they could congratulate them and chat more with them before they were scheduled to be at the airport, Mr. Pierce and Mr. Schaeffer smirked as they quietly walked past the duo and out of the room to give them some privacy.

Entranced by Shawn, Miriam lifted on her tippy

toes as his head lowered towards hers.

He searched her eyes, gauging to see if she wanted what he wanted. Her eyes darkened, and he knew, he hoped she was done fighting him. His lips were now inches away from hers. He moved in closer and nipped at her bottom lip.

She trembled but angled her head as she leaned into him.

He placed his hand on the small of her back and pulled her into him as his mouth covered hers.

Her arms instinctively wrapped around his neck.

Each kiss they shared told something new about them. The first kiss cemented their connection with one another. The kiss on the boat confirmed their safety and arousal of one another. This recent kiss confirmed they were meant to be.

Miriam moaned in his mouth and relaxed in his arms. He showed his approval by pulling her even closer to him and intensified the massaging of the nape of her neck.

Shawn used all his might to suspend his kiss with Miriam and pull away from her just enough to look into her eyes, but they were still closed. The pout of her lips suggested she was somewhat upset they had departed from kissing. "Mimi?"

"Yes?" She hesitantly opened her eyes.

"No more fighting me on us?"

"No, Shawn. You've shown me that I don't have

to."

He smiled wide. "That's right. I got you." His lips greedily covered hers as he palmed her butt.

Free of her inhibitions and knowing the other gentlemen were no longer in the room, she seized the moment, the kiss, by jumping up and straddling him. Shawn didn't waiver in securing her in his arms. He showed her yet again that he indeed had her.

Two months later....

"Mimi, babe, don't you think it's time to go and see her, or at least call and talk to her?"

"Um, do I have to?" she asked, pulling her feet under her on his couch as she leaned further into his side.

"With the way you've been rehearsing your speech the past month, I think you've been ready to."

"I am, I guess. I've always wanted to make amends with her, have a healthy relationship with her, even though I've done nothing wrong, but time and time again, she never crosses the bridge I try to build between us."

"I know, and I can only imagine what you've gone through concerning her over the years. But if there's one thing I've learned about you is that you're not a quitter. Within the two months since your promotion, you've built a team to handle the construction and engineering for Mr. Schaeffer's hotels and you have secured two more multi-million-dollar contracts for Pierce Industries. There is no stopping you woman, so don't hold back in trying to mend your relationship with your mother."

"You're right. I'll try to call her." She sat upright on the couch, grabbed her phone and pressed her mother's contact number.

Shawn kissed her lips and squeezed her knee right before her mother picked up.

"Huh-hello?"

Miriam shook her head. Her mother's slurred greeting made her acutely aware that she was drunk. Sadly, Miriam wasn't surprised that she was that way so early on the Saturday morning. Waking up to drink was Maxine's norm.

"Hello?"

"Hey, ma."

"Oh, so you finally decide to call me after what… how long has it been since we last talked?"

Miriam took a deep breath. As usual, Maxine wasted no time in berating her.

Tired of the insanely unhealthy merry-go-round she had been on with her mother for years, her eyes watered, and her heart rate sped up. She pulled the phone from her face, covered it with one hand, looked over at Shawn and said, "I can't do this right now. I've been so happy with work and you. I don't want this call with her to mess up the great energy around me."

"I know, Mimi, but your anger with her is why you freaked out on that drunk woman the other day who was cursing her daughter out in the store. You're still hurting because of her. Just give talking to her another try."

"Miriam," Maxine screamed through the phone. "Is that a man I hear with you? You better not get pregnant and ruin y'all lives." She sucked her teeth.

In spite of what she'd heard her mother just say and hating that Shawn was right, Miriam put her phone back up to her face in hopes of some type of reconciliation with Maxine.

"Ma, how have you been?"

"Fine," Maxine grunted. "Why are you calling me?"

Miriam heard the flicking of a lighter. Images surfaced of her mother blowing smoke in her face as a little girl as she stood nearby trying to gain her attention.

"I was just calling to talk to you. Ma, I would really like—"

"Dammit, Miriam, it's always about what you need, what you want. What about what I want? What about me? I had to sacrifice what I really wanted for you," she whined into the phone.

"Sacrifice? You never sacrificed anything for me. Thank God I was, but I didn't ask to be born." Miriam took a deep breath and lowered her voice. She had called her mother as a means to start afresh with her, but her mother's dismissal of her had made her slip back into the irate state she worked hard not to be in where she was concerned.

"In spite of past failed attempts to try and make things better with you, I decided to call you today in hopes that you would be a different woman, a better woman, but you know what, I give up trying to change you. Our relationship. You don't know anything about me, and you've never cared to. I've been chasing a position at my firm since I started there to prove something to you, but in reality, I only needed to prove something to myself to be happy."

Shawn squeezed her hand.

"I could've turned out any other way because of how little you cared for me growing up, but because I was misguided in seeking your approval, and more importantly, Ms. Rollins speaking life into me, I turned out to be who I am today." She stood up from the couch and began to pace the floor.

"You know, I've never even had a drink because I didn't want to end up like you." She shook her head and let out an angry chuckle. "Ma, I have a great man who takes me out and will drink water with me rather than make me feel uncomfortable by having a drink. That's crazy," she yelled and threw her free hand up in the air.

"I've come to realize that it's okay for me to drink socially if I want to because I would never allow myself to become what...what you've become." She took a deep breath to calm herself. It was not her intention to raise her voice, go off on her mother, but her constant cavalier attitude where she was concerned had her bubbling over.

Regardless of that, Maxine was still her mother and she felt she owed it to her not to holler at her. "Ma, no matter how much time I've spent over the years heartbroken that you never loved me, I really do love you." Having to admit yet again, out loud, that her mother never seemed to love her, normally gutted her, but this time, the thought, the words didn't sting so bad. She found herself smiling.

"I love you ma, and I hope that you truly get yourself together, but in the meantime, I'm going to move on with my life. I won't be doing things to try and gain your affection anymore. I'm living my life for me. I love you and I always will. Take care."

She didn't even bother to listen if her mother had a rebuttal or agreed with what she'd said, she was too busy amping up her smile and relishing in the knowledge that she was ready to live her life on her own terms.

"Come here." Shawn's crooked finger beckoned her towards him.

Staring at him, dancing in his seat, she giggled, eager to get to him to celebrate the burden she'd lifted off her shoulders when she stood her ground with her mother.

And when she sat on his lap and engaged him in a kiss, it was no game. He was her reality.

Other Books Available

Sisterhood Chronicles Series
Underneath It All
Discovery
Untold
When It Happens To You
All Things Considered

Forever Friends Series
Catch Me If You Can
It's Complicated

Limelight Series
Hues
Tones
Vision

Standalone Titles
After All Is Said & Done
The Bid Catcher: Distinguished Gentlemen Series

(Best if you read Forever Friends series before reading Sisterhood Chronicles 3)

ABOUT THE AUTHOR

Anita Davis is a former elementary teacher born and raised in Chicago. Although she wrote short stories much of her childhood, she didn't unlock and cultivate her passion as a writer until she became a writing teacher for middle school students. The more she had to create sample writings for her students, the more she realized her passion and ability to tell stories in the written form. She decided to hone her craft as a writer by completing her Master of Fine Arts in Creative Writing via National University. She now pursues writing books most of her time, in addition to being a flight attendant. Anita seeks to encourage, engage, and entertain her readers.

She is Co-Founder of Book Euphoria, a group of Chicago authors bound by their love of literature. Book Euphoria hosts literary events and they also founded the empowerment movement, Black Girl Passion.

Anita writes contemporary romantic women's fiction and seeks to encourage, engage, and entertain her readers.

authoranitadavis@gmail.com
www.authoranitadavis.com
Facebook: Anita Davis and Author page: Author Anita Davis
Instagram: @authoranitadavis   Twitter: @_AnitaDavis